THE
UNBANISHED

T. AARON CISCO

Dedicated to those who reject the notion that they are merely what others believe them to be...

Does the manner in which something dies outweigh the decision of whether or not to kill it? The abrupt termination of life should never be taken lightly and be avoided at all costs. The forceful taking of breath can also be a charitable gesture to alleviate further suffering, one in which allowing the creature to survive the encounter would be the true act of cruelty. The act of taking breath should be reserved only for instances in which no other options were available. This morning however, there was another option.

Although Orianne Duchamp wasn't squeamish, the sensation of the milky white grubs burrowing up through the soft mud beneath her knees and crawling over her heels was remarkably unpleasant. It had nearly broken her state of concentration. Dismissing distraction was a skill they had all worked to hone over the past thousand nights, but one she still had yet to master.

The howls of the forty-one other Youths in her Tutelage class filled the air as they broke formation and charged. Orianne was startled by the noise, but remained perspicaciously focused on both achieving her objective, and maintaining an acute awareness of her surroundings.

They faced east, towards the outer rim of the clearing, but their target had advanced on them from the south, catching them off guard. The unexpected turn of events set off a chain reaction of contagious chaos.

As the obstreperous display unfolded, Orianne raised her head for a better view. She watched her fellow Youths attacking without discipline, running around recklessly, throwing their weapons, and cursing when their haphazard aim failed to hit the target. She watched as the last of the Youths were knocked backwards across the grasses and thought back to her studies. The goal of this exercise was to assess their competency in tactical applications, but Orianne wasn't thinking of the numerous lectures regarding strategic offensives. Orianne instead thought back to the dialogues on convictions and merit.

Exhaling calmly, Orianne sprung from her position, drawing the ignited tip of her assegai along into the scaly trapezoidal head of the tauren lizard. The reptilian beast went rigid, then collapsed, its forked purple tongue dangling through its jagged rows of teeth.

The lizard's emerald eyes opened wide, then abruptly shut, as Orianne withdrew her spear. The wound had cauterized upon contact, and the smell of new charred flesh filled her nostrils. She stepped back, moving away from the unconscious reptile.

There was a beauty in the stillness of the creature. From the close vantage point, Orianne noticed that the tauren lizard's head was slightly smaller than the muscular neck and thickly armored, elongated body. The skin around its eyes was radiantly smooth. The rows of bony plates running down the serpentine spine glistened in the early light.

Mentor Alexandre emerged from behind the protective viewing screen on the far side of the clearing. He pulled the hood of his cloak over his head to protect his skin. Unlike the Youths, who possessed a spectrum of complexions ranging from dried oats to cephalopod ink, Alexandre's flesh contained no melanin. His flesh was highly sensitive to even the dim rays of the early morning light. He was followed by Malachi, the Associate Mentor, who dutifully, and somewhat begrudgingly, applauded as well.

"Well done, Orianne." Alexandre exclaimed, "I believe you are the first Youth to take life from the tauren lizard. Your fellow Youths were incapacitated. The beast was charging. You had a clear target. Why didn't you simply make the kill?"

"Mentor Alexandre," Orianne nodded in respect, twisting the handle of her assegai, extinguishing the ignited tip of the blade, "I remembered our lectures. The top of a tauren lizard's head is highly sensitive to temperature. The heat from my assegai overwhelmed those receptors, causing the creature to lose consciousness. And notice the lizard's scars. Though bred specifically for the purpose of these trainings, the lizard still deserves respect."

"You respect a tauren lizard?" Malachi raised an eyebrow. Some of the other Youths giggled softly.

"Why yes, Mentor Malachi." Orianne nodded, "It no more deserved to die for fulfilling its duties than any of us deserve to live for fulfilling our own. All life is valuable. While you question my empathy, I felt true compassion, and is compassion not one of the core tenets of our people?"

"Indeed, it is." Malachi conceded, "But the tauren lizard can heal itself from most any wound, even a mortal one. Can one truly share compassion for a life without end?"

"If one only one values life because it ends, then what one truly values is death, not life." Orianne replied.

"Hand of a hunter, heart of a healer, and the mind of a scholar." Alexandre smiled approvingly.

"Thank you, Mentor Alexandre." Orianne nodded, "As you have taught us, one must rely on the mind as much as the spear. Even more so perhaps."

"Indeed." Alexandre nodded, then turned to address the Youths, "Orianne has enabled your success. Return to your sleep-houses and prepare. The Ritual of Avenir will begin at full light, and tardiness will not be tolerated."

"As you have said it, so let it be so!" the Youths replied in well-trained, but enthusiastic unison.

Alexandre led the Youths back to the encampments that had been erected around the Skyfields. Though he kept a stoic expression, he walked with great pride. He noticed that Orianne also had changed her gait. Her usually hesitant steps had been replaced with confident strides.

The central region of Ardwood was known for its expansive forests with their lush canopies of densely clustered leaves and branches, that only allowed just enough light for a diversity of mushrooms and fungal cultures to flourish in the rich, charcoal grey soil, but the Skyfields were an endless ocean of green and beige grasses.

Along the edges of the massive clearing, tangling branches met swaying grasses. The fields were engirdled by gnarled roots, that bursts free from their subterranean cover to greedily bask in the rays of morning light. The sky above the plains stretched on for miles in every direction. At night, the unencumbered view of the heavens offered a breathtaking spectacle of countless stars.

A constant clamor of inhuman noises rumbled day and night. The crisp breezes cradled the beastly songs and disquieting shrieks, echoing through the air, blending in harmony with the comforting sounds of the thousands of souls who called Ardwood home.

Later in the day, as the sun reached the apex of its journey across the sky, Orianne was still overflowing with self-assuredness. Although her ceremonial garments were secondhand, they were impeccable. She took great care in keeping them in excellent condition. Even as she ate her small, savory lunch of yams and rice, she was careful not to let a single drop of sauce stain her linens.

As she wiped her mouth, a few errant strands of hair slipped from the bun atop her head. The newly liberated locks brushed against the contours of her face. She carried herself with the mature reserve of those far older, but fixated on her meal, she was as fresh-faced as any Youth.

She noticed Alexandre staring at her from a distance and scrunched her nose. It was a playful but respectful acknowledgement of their bond. He returned her smile and took a seat next to her. As she dipped her fingers in the cleansing bowl, she noticed her reflection and sighed quietly, watching her face ripple in the water.

Orianne's relationship with her recognition marks was complicated. She was proud of her achievements, but also resentful as they were proof that her physicality was valued more than her intellect. Rows of small white spots curved beneath her eyes, around her lips, and ran down the center of her nose and chin. All earned during her Tutelage, they identified her as the most skilled among peers.

The most conspicuous and impressive sign of her abilities was The Mark of Three Moons. The collection of concentric rings sat prominently in the center of her forehead. The highly coveted accolade was rarely bestowed upon anyone, let alone a Youth still under Tutelage. It was ironic that someone who worked so hard to avoid drawing attention, was the most deserving of it.

Orianne rubbed her eyes and yawned while gazing out over the clearing. Every three thousand nights, Youths that successfully completed Tutelage, gathered together in the Skyfields for the Ritual of Avenir. The outcome of the ceremony was of the greatest importance. Within a few moments, the Youths would pledge themselves to one of the four Stratums: Vaincre, Explorateur, Enlightenment, and Unir. Upon approval, they would be accepted and recognized as a full member of society with all the privileges- and obligations- that entailed.

Alexandre and Orianne had both dreamt of this day since they were infants. Alexandre had completed the Ritual of Avenir two seasons ago. Pledging Explorateur, he rose through the rank swiftly, earning the position of Chief Mentor in a few hundred nights. He was ecstatic that his dear friend was now ready to pledge. But now that the time had finally arrived, it looked as though Orianne wanted the sun to fall from the sky.

"Is everything all right, Orianne?" Alexandre asked, "Were the yams and herbs not to your liking?"

Orianne smiled weakly. She was a few hundred nights younger than Alexandre, but they were closer than family.

"No, Alexandre," Orianne shook her head, "It's not the yams. The yams were delicious, as always."

"Perhaps you're worried that some vile creature will descend from Umadyn?" Alexandre chuckled.

"No." Orianne shook her head.

"If any monsters dare to come into the Skyfields of Ardwood," Alexandre teased, "They'll be handled."

"I'm just nervous." Orianne pushed him away playfully.

"Why are you of all people nervous?" Alexandre asked, "There is no question that you were the best!"

"That's just it." Orianne inhaled deeply, "I worry that they're going to stick me with the haughty Aristos in Courbonne. Perhaps I performed *too* well."

"Never apologize for your excellence!" Alexandre's voice was stern yet caring, "Everyone knows you have physical skills, yes? But everyone also knows that you are brilliant. You wish to serve the Enlightenment Stratum in Navanca? You are qualified to serve there. You've earned the right to serve there. So that's where you'll go."

"I'm not so sure." Orianne sighed, "Yes, I petitioned all the Mentors individually, but…"

"Orianne Duchamp!" a booming voice soaked in unrestrained authority rang out behind them.

Orianne and Alexandre turned their heads. Squinting in the morning light, they gazed upon the imposing and impressively graceful silhouette of Zamaya Bellegarde.

Her poise alone commanded unwavering respect. Rows of commendation marks covered Zamaya's face and forehead. The base of her elegant neck was encircled by intricately concentric rings of cicatrices, honorable scarification marks that had been earned over a career of triumphs spanning two generations.

Her appearance- though captivating- was her least impressive feature. Unlike the more delicate leaders who served alongside her in the Unir Stratum, Zamaya was not one to dictate and delegate from afar. Her authority had been earned in, and confirmed by, an extensive record of blood, fire, and leading from the front.

"Mother Bellegarde." Alexandre bowed his head in deference, "It is an honor."

Zamaya politely stepped around the wooden table to face them, so they wouldn't have to squint.

"Chief Mentor Alexandre," Zamaya's voice was throaty, rich, and measured, "May I have a word with you?"

"Of course."

Alexandre nodded politely to Orianne, excusing himself from the table. Zamaya escorted him a few steps away, just out of Orianne's earshot. Their conversation was brief, and hard to discern. Alexandre's calm demeanor was present, but compared to the dispassionate discipline of Zamaya, his occasional head nods and eyebrow raises appeared almost comically exaggerated.

Orianne sat up straighter in her chair when they returned to the table. Alexandre took a seat next to Orianne. She stole a quick glance at his face, but his flat expression revealed nothing about the conversation. Zamaya lowered her gaze and inspected Orianne's commendation marks.

"It is an honor!" Orianne gasped, her discomfort replaced by humiliation at her outburst, "Please forgive me for speaking out of turn. I meant no disrespect."

"Pay it no mind." Zamaya chuckled, "It will not be long before you will have a Stratum and a title. I think we can excuse a few moments of premature informality."

"Thank you for understanding." Orianne exhaled sheepishly, "How can I be of service?"

"I was hoping you could answer a riddle?" Zamaya responded, gracefully pushing aside her striped capelet as she took a seat across from Orianne.

"I will do my best." Orianne nodded.

"The Chief Mentor speaks quite highly of you." Zamaya smiled, "Your record in the field exercises is exemplary. I even saw the account you wrote on the origins of our Stratums. It was remarkable."

"She is the best of her peers." Alexandre piped up, "Just this morning during the last trials, she neutralized the tauren lizard without killing it."

"Impressive indeed," Zamaya continued, "Orianne, you're so young, yet your marks nearly match my own. Why would someone of your prowess, claim intent for the Enlightenment Stratum?"

"Well, I—" Orianne stammered.

"You and I both bear the mark of the Three Moons." Zamaya interrupted, "Why waste those skills in Navanca?"

"Wasted?" Orianne recoiled.

"With respect," Alexandre sucked in his breath, "As I informed your just now, I don't feel that her talents would be wasted in Navanca. She wishes to serve by raising the next generations to be strong of both body *and* mind."

"I was not speaking to you, Mentor." Zamaya glared at Alexandre, "Orianne, I am not asking to disparage our noble sisters in Navanca, but simply seeking to understand your motivations. Can you provide me the clarification I seek?"

"I just..." Orianne began, "I want to be seen as more."

"I see." Zamaya smirked, "Those who serve within the Enlightenment Stratum are the reason why all of us are able to do what we do. Every soul of Javari owe their lives to their teachings. But there are many who are capable in that capacity. There are not so many who could do what you do. This is why, on this Ritual of Avenir, and all those going forward, you will join me."

"But—" Orianne peeped, but quickly remembered her station. Though she was shocked, she knew better than to speak against the great Zamaya Bellegarde.

"No one Stratum is greater than the others. We are all one people, yes?" Zamaya arched an eyebrow, "I can see my words aren't enough to convince you."

"I'm sorry." Orianne lowered her head.

"Stand!" Zamaya stood from the table.

"I don't understand." Alexandre asked, throwing a worried look at Orianne, "Have we offended you? When we spoke, I thought--"

"Silence Mentor! Or I will tear out your throat" Zamaya roared, "Orianne, I command you to stand!"

Orianne and Alexandre exchanged glances. They both knew that something terrible was coming, but Orianne was still a Youth, and had to obey.

"Yes." Orianne stood.

"Come around the table and stand by me." Zamaya ordered, inhaling slowly. With a battle cry that startled even the black herons soaring above, Zamaya unleashed a frenzied barrage of slashing chops and cross punches.

Orianne was thrown back by the blows, but quickly regained her footing, raising her forearms and knees to deflect the onslaught of palm strikes and elbow thrusts.

"Please stop!" Orianne cried, "I do not understand."

"If you wish to join the Enlightenment Stratum, then subdue me!" Zamaya bellowed, landing a hooked fist.

"I am a Youth! I will not strike you!" Orianne reared back, crossing her arms to defend herself. She focused on Zamaya's pummeling combinations, trying to anticipate the next punch. She ducked, narrowly avoiding what would've been a devastating heel kick to the jaw.

Orianne ducked and swung her left knee, knocking the legs out from under Zamaya. Before her back hit the ground, Zamaya rebounded with an expertly executed handspring, landing in a low squat. She rocked side to side rhythmically, slowly. Snarling, she extended her hands with open palms, her feet planted firmly in the soil.

"Impressive, Orianne." Zamaya smiled, "But far from perfect, as I'm sure your newly acquired contusions can attest. Yes, you are still a Youth, but that is no reason for you to hold back when being attacked."

"With respect." Orianne wheezed, "You are Zamaya Bellegarde. You are first among the living. Yet I haven't even completed the Ritual of Avenir."

"I am slighted!" Alexandre jumped to his feet, interrupting their exchange defiantly.

"What?!" Zamaya snarled at him.

"As both Chief Mentor, and an honored Venturer of the Explorateur Stratum, I am slighted. Zamaya Bellegarde, you have assaulted a Youth under my mentorship. By rules of decorum, we have a quarrel."

"Quarrel?" Zamaya snickered, "With me?"

"Alexandre!" Orianne cried, "What are you doing?"

"What is right." Alexandre answered unsteadily.

All the Youths in the fields of Ardwood stared in amazement. Even the other Mentors put aside their parchments to bear witness. That there was a captive audience was not lost on Zamaya.

"Youth and Mentors of Ardwood!" Zamaya proclaimed, "Hear my voice. I am the Puissant Haute Champion of Javari. I have been accused of offense against this Venturer, and as such we now have a quarrel."

"Alexandre..." Orianne's voice trembled with fright.

"By rule of decorum this quarrel may be settled either through bloodshed or by decree." Zamaya exclaimed, "As such, I decree the quarrel settled, and the offense moot."

You cannot!" Alexandre yelled astonished.

"As Puissant Haute Champion of Javari, I am the person of highest station present. To issue decree is a privilege of my station is it not?"

"As you have said it, so let it be done." Alexandre spat.

"Mind the tone of your tongue, Venturer." Zamaya menacingly stared him down.

"Mother Bellegarde," Orianne pleaded, "I have already petitioned the Mentors with a statement of intent."

"I've watched your progress through Tutelage." Zamaya turned back to Orianne, "I've read your accounts, and seen the progress records. I'm well aware of your intent, but I'm also aware of your gifts. Those gifts would be better served taking life *from our* enemies rather than teaching Youths *about our* enemies. Visitants steal our crops. Beasts from Umadyn and Ayrsulth ravage the countryside. Javari cannot bloom in the shadow of fear. Your role in diminishing that fear would be a great one. The stories of your triumphs will inspire a hundred generations, and is inspiration not an effective tool of instruction?"

"Mother Bellegarde, I serve Javari, but I will not shed blood. How many souls, in every region, across generations are lost to violence? Like you, I seek to better our--"

"You are nothing like me." Zamaya scoffed, "You are wasting your talents. Perhaps your Mentors condone such a squandering of gifts, but I'm not one to dismiss potential so readily. Or is it something else?"

"Mother Bellegarde?" Orianne sputtered.

"Yes," Zamaya nodded, "That's it. You're not opposed to taking breath. You're just afraid. You've honed your skills, but you're drowning in a sea of cowardice."

"I am not a coward." Orianne snarled.

"You want Navanca? Then fight for it."

"Orianne, are you okay?" Alexandre whispered.

"Yes." Orianne whispered back, nodding sternly, "As you said earlier, I should not apologize for my excellence."

"Are my terms understood?" Zamaya asked smugly.

"Yes." Orianne angrily spat back. Her honor had been questioned. Her friend had been insulted; his life threatened. In the moment, the vaunted status and reputation of Zamaya meant nothing.

"Excellent." Zamaya smiled, "Let's begin."

Zamaya repeated her deafening battle cry and charged Orianne. Their bodies collided, knocking over tables, sending the dishes flying.

Their arms and legs were arrows of flesh. Every attack was answered in kind. Falling into the long grass of the Skyfields, their bodies coiled and constricted. Though Orianne was younger and faster, Zamaya was far more experienced and cunning.

Zamaya's hands emerged from the fracas, outmaneuvering her young opponent's rudimentary holds and strikes. Twisting around, Zamaya locked Orianne's left elbow against the natural bend of the joint, then wrapped her other hand firmly around Orianne's windpipe.

Though she couldn't inhale easily, Orianne's kept going. As long as she was consciousness, she wouldn't allow herself to yield. Her blows still landed, but the longer Zamaya squeezed, the less effective her attacks became.

Orianne locked eyes with Alexandre. Alexandre inhaled slowly, imploring the ancestral gods to allow Orianne's diminishing will to feed off his own resolve. Orianne began to feel lightheaded and was fading fast.

Summoning the last remnants of tenacity, Orianne jerked her arm back against her entrapped elbow. The splintering crack was so loud it startled Zamaya into releasing her grip. The reprieve was momentary, but enough for Orianne to inhale unobstructed. The shock from breaking her own arm provided enough of a boost to throw her fearsome opponent off balance.

Orianne assumed a dominant position, straddling Zamaya with her knees pinning down her shoulders. Zamaya thrashed about but couldn't find leverage to wriggle out from underneath. Orianne stared into Zamaya's eyes, leaned down and placed the point of her good elbow between Zamaya's nose and upper lip.

"Cede now," Orianne snarled through ragged breath.

"Cede?" Zamaya smirked.

"Cede now!" Orianne barked, "I swear by the elders, I will lunge down and take your teeth. I have bested you in combat. I have won the quarrel! Now cede!"

"You haven't won." Zamaya laughed haughtily, "You've merely rendered one of your limbs useless."

"One of my limbs is useless, yes." Orianne's eyes raged defiantly, "But only *one*. I've immobilized *all* of yours. This quarrel is over. I've won."

"Have you?" Zamaya mockingly chuckled.

Orianne unleashed a primal roar. Rearing back, she prepared to crush Zamaya's obstinate grin. Suddenly, a sharp pain exploded through her body. Orianne looked down to see the bloodied tip of a short spear jutting out from her chest. The blade slid back slowly. Sliding backwards, through her lungs and out of the meat of her back. The agony was more than Orianne could bear.

Orianne collapsed in distress, shocked by the sight of the blade being held by a long black tail curling out from underneath Zamaya's robe.

"Oh, Orianne." Zamaya loomed, the tail brandishing the short spear behind her, "Did my status slip your mind? Many gifts are bestowed upon those from Courbonne."

"But…" Orianne's gasps were bare audible.

"Metamorphosis is one of the most coveted Magycs reserved for a select few who serve the Unir Stratum." Zamaya shook her head, withdrawing the spear, and her tail, back under her tunics. "I'm sure now it will be many thousands of nights before you forget."

"Orianne!" Alexandre cried out in horror. He ran to her. Dropping to his knees, he cradled his young protégé, "How dare you use your gifts against a Youth! The Bronze Chieftain outlawed the use of Magycs against--- "

"Silence yourself, Venturer! Who are you to speak on behalf of the Bronze Chieftain!" Zamaya raised her arms. A geyser of red and gold flames erupted from her hands. Coiling tongues of blue-black smoke encircled her as the enchanted blaze shot heavenward, filling the clearing with a bewitching light brighter than the morning sky.

Alexandre, along with every Youth and Mentor in the Skyfields, dropped to their knees, bent forward, and pressed their foreheads against the dirt.

"Forgive us, Mother Zamaya!" Alexandre cried "We beg for leniency. Please do not let my momentary arrogance condemn all the Youth!"

Zamaya clenched her fists and threw her arms down. The fire of the Magycs expanded in a massive cloud of flames. It swept through the clearing, washing over the gathering, incinerating every Youth and Mentor where they knelt, leaving nothing but effigies of ash and despair in its roaring wake. The blaze dissipated, leaving only Zamaya, Alexandre, and the wounded body of Orianne unscathed.

"Rise, Alexandre." Zamaya purred, "Carry your protégé to my caravan, and place her in my palanquin."

"She needs healing! Is she now to die a Youth?" Alexandre could barely contain his anger, though he was smart enough to mask his contempt, "She was willing to fight, and now you take her breath?"

"Calm yourself." Zamaya shook her head, "I would not squander one so talented. I have a gourd of coppermilk in my caravan. As of this moment, she is no longer a Youth. I hereby grant her the title of Instructor. I will take her to Navanca and officially establish her position."

"What of the Youth who no longer draw breath?"

"Oh, Mentor Alexandre." Zamaya let out a cruel laugh. Raising her arms again, the ashen remains of the dead were miraculously restored to their living entities.

"But…" Alexandre stammered.

"Miragem is also one of the Magycs I wield. Your reality, and perception thereof, is what I decide it to be This was merely a warning."

"Yes, Mother Zamaya." Alexandre bowed his head in shame, embarrassed and defeated, he mumbled meekly "But what of my protégé?"

"She will carry the title of Instructor, but she will ride with the Vaincre, for an upcoming expedition."

"The Vaincre?" Alexandre replied alarmed, "But they journey deep within Ayrsulth, battling all manner of beasts to retrieve coppermilk and--"

"Yes." Zamaya nodded, "And there are many expeditions that could benefit from the inclusion of an Instructor with such remarkable combat skills. If you have parting words for your friend, now is the time. There is no more for us to discuss."

"As you have said it, so let it be so."

Alexandre carried Orianne to the Zamaya's palanquin and laid her inside. He found the small gourd of coppermilk, pulled the top, and held it to Orianne's lips. The enchanted elixir healed her arm and repaired her chest wound. She opened her eyes and looked up at Alexandre.

"Alexandre?" she coughed, "What happened? What is the result of the quarrel?"

"You were victorious, but not triumphant." Alexandre squeezed her shoulder, tears welling in his pale eyes.

"What does that mean?" Orianne asked, tears spilling from her own wide eyes.

"You will go to Navanca to be officially instated as an Instructor. But when your wounds fully heal, you will be sent to Tolerbella, and assigned to an expedition."

"I should've held back in Tutelage." Orianne sighed.

"No!" Alexandre sniffed, and put on an air of confidence for his lifelong friend, "As I said before, never apologize for your excellence."

"It is time." Zamaya called out.

"Goodbye my friend." Alexandre hugged Orianne tightly, then stepped away from the palanquin.

Orianne dropped her head onto the suede cushions of the seats. Struggling to withhold her tears, she silently made a vow of vengeance against Zamaya.

-TUTELAGE LESSON: PROGENITORS-

One should always refrain from decrepitude and timidity. Above all, shelter yourself and your kinfolk from iniquity of deed, and the illicit pursuits born of arrogant thought. Our Progenitors did not curse us with the spirit of carnality, but rather of forbearance and abundance. Through the good of the whole, the one shall be sheltered from devastation, and bask in triumphant prosperity.

The gulf between determination and delirium is both infinite and invisible. The poetry of the damned often falls on deaf ears. The will of a people may echo for miles without answer. But faith can only be deemed folly in the hindsight of forfeit. Seven thousand generations ago, the Progenitors labored tirelessly to build a thriving civilization. The results of their onerous burden took root and spread to the furthest shores.

Through procreation and exploration, they blanketed the lush and fruitful continent. They named their world Javari, in tribute to Queen Chief Sauvanne Figuier Javari, the fallen matriarch who freed them from bondage, braved the endless depths of the Fleshwater Ocean, and led them through the unfathomable to set foot upon their new homelands.

Tens of thousands of nights passed as they matured and prospered, building a complex and relatively equitable society. For the first few hundred generations, they lived in benevolent harmony with the mystical indigenous creatures, all of whom were wonderous and beautifully necessary to the prosperity of the land, in their own distinctive ways.

The kongamato gave them meat and building materials. They learned what crops to eat, what fields to plow, and how to safely avoid the hazards of chacals and carcolhs. They learned to forge weapons and build ships. They mastered the strategies of conquest by studying the hunting tactics of the gbahali, and migration patterns of the leviathans.

Then the Visitants arrived from across the oceans, travelling some ninety-one nights, seeking to empower themselves in the name of their own cursed homelands. The lands from which they came possessed a few natural resources, but nowhere near the abundant array of plants and animals, of fine minerals and raw materials. They were also wholly devoid of preternatural knowledge and had no comprehension of the Magycs.

The Visitants carried with them strange armaments and advanced technologies, but their deadliest weapon was unseen to the Progenitors. There was a pox in their blood. One for which there was no remedy, and one that threatened to decimate not only the stricken Visitants, but all life on Javari.

The Bronze Chieftain, the Iron, and Gold chieftains, the elders, along with the Queenmothers and Mentors from all the regions, along with the beings from Ayrsulth, gathered to discuss the Visitant issue. They didn't want to let them die, but at the same time, could not endanger their own peoples. They decided that the Visitants, with their frail biology, ignorance of the natural ways, and crippling foreign sickness, could stay in the coastal region along the Southern border of Courbonne, just a few nights journey north of Navanca. The Visitants agreed, thankful for the merciful generosity of the Javari people.

At first, the arrangement worked. The Visitants stayed in their area, receiving instructions on how to work the land, grow food, and build shelter. Emissaries from their enclave were allowed to travel to other regions to learn necessary skills. But the emissaries would return to their enclaves, with stories of the splendor of the other regions, and after two generations, the Visitants became covetous. They gazed upon the magnificent people of Tolerbella, Ardwood, Navanca, and Courbonne, and devised plans to conquer the continent.

The Progenitors from the region known as Courbonne defeated the Visitant forces using their knowledge of the Magycs. The survivors were exiled to a narrow band of land between Terre d'Os and Terre de Sang. It was far from the coastal waters, and regularly beset upon by picots and carcolhs. Even when the monsters were held at bay, the terrain itself was suitable for little more than basic survival and necessary sustenance, but the alternative was death.

Celebrated as heroes, the leaders of Courbonne then established the strict social hierarchy known as the Stratums, to maintain power and order, and defend against any potential threat from the Visitants or Magyc creatures. And this is the way it was and the way it continues to be, but a single truth still yet stands

Trust in the Stratums while rejecting depravity and disobedience; and in this way, whatever has begun, can never be undone.

-2-

The air was crisp, the trees were dead, and the clouds were full of demons. Every member of the expedition knew that there was a good chance they'd never reach their destination, yet they climbed anyway. The inevitable lack of success didn't slow their pace. Neither cold winds, nor cold facts, deterred their ambitions. The decrepit jaws of failure would only bare their fangs if they stopped moving. Night after night, they trudged on through the frozen peaks of Ayrsulth, across terrain unsuitable for any and all who still drew breath. Still, they climbed.

On the eve of the forty second morning of the journey, they reached a soft plateau. The raspy shrieks of the farfadet swarm echoed off the hardened mud of the mountain path. Though her body and mind had been pushed far beyond their limits, Orianne felt the same calmingly intense feeling as she had facing the tauren lizard.

The farfadets beat their leathery wings with a chaotic atonal rhythm, as their tails thrashed about in an ominously percussive cacophony, a thousand feet above the expedition group. The first two farfadets that the expedition had noticed the previous night hadn't left. They'd merely gone to fetch the rest of the hive.

Farfadets had darkly diaphanous wings. Their wide faces were ringed with tiny horns that shone like newly polished silver. The serrated protrusions running the length of their prehensile tails sliced flesh and iron with equally effortless precision. Their comparatively small size made them almost adorable, but with their teeth bared, all winsome pretenses were completely washed away.

"Ready your assegai!" the booming voice of Skinner Hakim Jarrah commanded.

After all the nights following his lead, Orianne was still in awe of him. He was older than most of the Elders- only a few thousand nights younger than the Bronze Chieftain herself- but just like fermented starch root becomes more intoxicating the longer it's stored, his advanced age had only made him more formidable.

It had been forty thousand nights since he'd earned the rank of Skinner, the highest echelon of the Vaincre Stratum. He'd had offers to join the Elders but had no interest in pursuing the sedentary life of a politician.

Hakim was unwaveringly devoted to Tolerbella, as well as the Vaincre creed; *a cautious life lacks purpose.* To him, that was more than an adage. It was a personal oath of lifelong defiance. Hakim was the only one who didn't carry an ignited assegai. Instead, he brandished the Almighty Hellreaver, a dual-bladed scimitar made of ebonsteel.

The elongated hilt was wrapped in black twine and goat leather. The fore blade was broad enough to sever an opponent in two with a single stroke. The hind-blade was curved and twisted, offering both protection from, and devastating offense toward, anyone foolish enough to attempt a rear attack. It was an exceptional weapon for an exceptional fighter, as dangerous as the man who wielded it.

The frontline of the expedition stood shoulder to shoulder alongside Hakim. The expedition group had been deployed in two parallel formations. All eighty of the frontline bore the markings of the Schemer Class, the mid-tier of the Vaincre Stratum. They were disciplined and lean. Every one of them anxious and eager to take a life, or give their own, without hesitation.

The warriors in the front would spark the initial engagement, buying time and cutting down the first forces of the opposition, while the rear fighters lie in wait, holding off until the perfect moment to strike with an overwhelmingly ferocious second wave.

The two-hundred rear and reserve guardians behind the frontline were equally menacing. Though most of them had never before engaged nonhuman combatants, as members of the Searcher Class, the lowest tier of the Vaincre Stratum, they were eager to prove their merits through bloodshed.

Orianne stayed close to the reserve guardians in the back. She was well aware of how unfavorable her presence on the expedition had been. The Schemers in particular had been explicit in their desire to open her veins and leave her corpse rotting on the mountain path.

She was the only one who wasn't of the Vaincre Stratum. Two thousand, one hundred and ninety nights had passed since the time of her Tutelage, facing Zamaya at the Ritual of Avenir, and now she was a model member of the Instructor Class from the Enlightenment Stratum. Though experienced and well-versed in her studies, she suspected that the only reason she'd lasted on the expedition for as long as she had, was because she had been placed by Zamaya Bellegarde. But that protection was precarious. In the heat of battle, it would be easy for the ignited tip of a Searcher's spear to find its way into the meat of her chest.

The threats weren't just external. The expedition had become susceptible to the Visitant pox. The signs of infection had first revealed themselves a few nights ago during the most arduous part of their ascent.

The afflicted spent the first hours after contraction coughing and groaning. By sun-fall, the disease left them practically immobilized, drenched in perspiration, lying prone on their backs, screaming about the agonizing sensations radiating from their being.

While most of the sick banged their fists against themselves in a futile attempt to drive out the pain, others scratched and clawed at their limbs, digging deep into their own flesh, searching in vain for any relief from the agony. By the time the sky fully darkened, all were blinded from exhaustion. Broken and dehydrated, leaking urine, blood, and bile, they drew their last breaths as the foreign-born virus overwhelmed them completely.

They'd started this expedition with over five thousand. Now, only six hundred remained. Glancing at the ominous sky, listening to the cries of the farfadets circling above, Orianne began to envy those who'd succumbed to horrific complications of the devastating pox.

"In all my travels Orianne, I've never seen a swarm such as this." Asa Gabo whispered, "Have you?"

She'd only drawn breath for sixty-nine hundred nights, but Asanda's skills as a Searcher were already legendary. Her inexperience had prevented her from ascending to the role of Schemer, but there was no question that she'd be granted a higher station if she survived the expedition.

"Only in the writings during my Tutelage." Orianne whispered back, "For this many farfadets to gather in one place, we must be close to the central chambers of the hive."

"Indeed." Asa nodded, "I will do my best to protect you, but if and when the moment comes, ignite your staff and aim for their eyes. Beware their tails and try to draw them in close. Try to direct their talons towards the fleshier parts of your body, yes? But be mindful of their heel spurs and talons. It does not take much farfadet poison to take life from the most hardened Skinners. Understood?"

"Venom."

"What's that?"

"You said farfadet poison. Farfadets have venom. Venom is given. Poison is taken. Something bites you and you die, that means venomous. If you instead you bite something and died from the meat, that means poisonous."

"I forget sometimes that you are of the Enlightenment Stratum." Asa chuckled, "Poisonous. Venomous. Whichever it is, just try not to get slashed, understood?"

"Yes Asa."

Orianne twisted the ignition band of her assegai. The top half of the spear glowed with soft white light. She glanced at the pattern painted on the hilt- two black stripes, three white- representing her home region of Navanca, and silently wondered if she'd ever see it again.

"Don't be afraid, Orianne." Asa smiled grimly, "Relish the next few moments. If these are to be our final breaths, then it's best not to waste them on fear."

Orianne watched as Asa and the others readied their ngunis- oval shields made from bolts of bone-weave and iron. She looked down at her own nguni. There wasn't even a scratch in the patchwork tapestry of kongamato wing skin pulled over the frame of pressed windwood.

Back when the Progenitors solidified their claim to the Javari continent, they'd slain the indigenous kongamato to fashion ngunis. The shields were able to withstand the metal blades and foreign fury of the invading Visitant forces. Orianne's shield hadn't felt the defiant strike of an enemy's sword, nor the raging slash of a monster's claw. She quietly prayed that the ancient defenses would still protect her now, hundreds of generations later.

Glancing down, Orianne noticed something odd about the shadow cast by her nguni. Curious, she slipped the tortoise shell bracer off of her arm and placed her bare wrist against the dirt. At this time of day, at this altitude, the ground should be damp, semi-soft, and warm. But the soil she felt was hard, dry, and cool against her exposed skin. Rifling through the cache of knowledge she'd gained through her Tutelage, she realized with horror what those conditions represented.

Panicking, she dashed to the head of the formation, pushing until she reached the first ranks of the frontline. Skinner Hakim was surrounded by an imposing ring of captains, one foot braced against a rotting stump, as he chewed on a handful of weevil larvae called akokono.

"Skinner Hakim!" she called out, steadying her nerves, "May I have a word, please?"

Hakim raised an eyebrow, but not his head. He nodded in acknowledgement of her voice and motioned to his captains to make space. He furrowed his wide brow as he swallowed the last bites of the akokono. It was undoubtedly flavorless, but sustenance was a necessity.

"Instructor Orianne." Hakim nodded.

"Skinner Hakim, my apologies, but it is imperative that I speak with you now."

"More infections among the ranks?" he asked, swallowing the last bites of his akokono.

"No, not that I'm aware of." Orianne shook her head, "I'm afraid it's far more urgent."

"Well then, speak." he commanded, his tone slightly annoyed. The captains eyed her with open disdain.

"Skinner Hakim," she spoke cautiously, "I am not an experienced Searcher or Schemer. I am merely the Instructor assigned to this expedition."

"This I know." Hakim snorted.

"Though young, I am fully qualified to assess every aspect of our journey," Orianne continued, "and keep you informed of any developments that may negatively impact the pursuit of our objective. I do not mean to offend or undermine your leadership, but it is my duty to offer counsel, based on my informed observations, to the fullest extent of my abilities."

"Orianne," he sighed loudly, "Just say your piece."

"We must turn back. The Time of Verglas is upon us."

"Turn back?" Hakim stood, his captains parted fully until they were all standing behind him, "You Instructors are far too academic. Learn to look with your eyes- not your mind. The coppermilk surely must be near, which means the Veil must be near, yet you suggest abandonment?"

Orianne swallowed hard and inhaled sharply. She knew that her next words would have to be extremely precise.

"I would never suggest that we abandon our duties." she bowed her head even lower, "But considering how far we have travelled and the conditions of the weather, the best course of action would be to retreat before it's too late to descend to a safer position on the mountainside."

"The best course!" Hakim roared, "In addition to the thousands among our expedition, more thousands have died searching these mountains, trying in vain to find the Veil of Bone, to end our dependence on coppermilk?"

"Yes, Skinner Hakim." Orianne demurred, "I'm aware."

"Have you seen the infirmed journey to Courbonne, only to find there was no coppermilk to be spared?" Hakim continued, "Have you heard the cries of the desperate? Have you felt the anguish of the dying? We owe it to them, and our own sense of duty and decency. This is not the time for cautious deliberation. It is a time for action!"

"Skinner Hakim, I meant no disrespect." Orianne dropped to her knees, pleading earnestly, "I am not suggesting we end the expedition, but rather hold off until the conditions are less hazardous."

"Less hazardous?" Hakim laughed.

"I implore you, Skinner Hakim." Orianne cried, "We've lost so many already, and soon it will not be safe for any of us. We should wait—"

"Wait until it's more comfortable?!" Hakim laughed, "This is not one of the symposium lounges in Navanca. Your comfort is far from a priority."

"Skinner Hakim, I only meant to—"

"No!" Skinner Hakim bellowed, "Speak no more! The impending melee is merely a herald of things to come. Just a blood-soaked aperitif for the brutal feast that undoubtedly awaits us. Girded and ready, our bones will bend, our flesh will bruise, but so long as my heart beats, and the morning light cast rays upon my old soul, surrender is not an option."

"But Skinner…"

"Do not test my patience any further, Instructor. You will return to your station at the rear, or I will have my captains cast you off the side of this mountain, where you may take your chances with gravity."

"Skinner Hakim," Orianne hung her head, "I am only trying to save us."

"So am I." Hakim snarled.

"As you have said it, so let it be so." Orianne acquiesced.

Orianne quickly stood and ran back to her position at the rear, ignoring the stares of the ranks as she pushed past them again. When she resumed her station, she dropped to her knees and felt the dirt again, hoping she was mistaken. The dirt was still cold. The path was still hard.

A rear guardian suffering from the early stages of the Visitant pox coughed and spat out a dark globule of phlegm. The tar-like mucus landed inches from Orianne's feet, reminding her of the diagrams of black beetle mushrooms from her homeopathic studies. The high-altitude fungi were often used to add strong, spicy flavors to bland dishes.

Her eyes widened as she recalled that when consumed whole, black beetle mushrooms could also incite fever. It wouldn't be enough to stem the full brunt of the Verglas, but if she could find enough of them, and convince the warriors to eat them, it might buy more time.

"What are you doing?" Asa whispered.

"Searching for black beetle mushrooms."

"Are you hungry?" Asa chuckled, "You crave spicy fungus, when the farfadets could descend at any moment?"

"I'm trying to prepare for the Verglas." Orianne whispered back, continuing her frantic digging.

"Orianne," Asa sighed with exasperation, "The weather is the least of our concerns. Stand tall before the--"

Asa's last statement hung in the air unresolved, as her throat burst open, spraying hot blood across Orianne's startled face. The grisly, crimson shower sent her reeling backwards, stumbling in the brittle mountain grass. Asa's head flew from her shoulders, bouncing off the grimy, blood-stained under-tunic of her armor, before rolling to a stop in the dirt by Orianne's knee.

"Farfadets descending!" a rear guardian screamed.

The entire swarm swooped down from the rear. Dozens of farfadets quickly began making brutal work of the expedition. The rest of the team were too engaged with the swarm's surprise rear attack to notice Asanda's demise.

The heads of the hunting hyenas were bisected. The supply donkeys were disemboweled. The messenger birds were eviscerated in their cages. The torturous demise that befell the support beasts was nothing compared to the nightmarish horrors unleased upon the expedition ranks.

A group of farfadets surrounded Kofi Darwish, the mahogany-skinned son of legendary Explorateurs, Wajid and Raina. The farfadets tore the skin from his face and neck. His eyes pleaded for mercy, which was granted when a farfadet buried its talons in his throat.

Amandine Thibault, Hakim Jarrah's second in command who led the rear guardians, was completely covered in the winged abominations. The corpses of a half dozen farfadets dropped, but for each one killed, two more came to replace them. Amandine was a remarkably large woman with gloriously intricate tattoos adorning her shaved head.

She kept her calloused hands wrapped tightly around her assegai, swinging it expertly at the oncoming creatures, refusing to yield any ground even as they flayed her body where she stood. She finally succumbed when a single farfadet inserted its talons into her mouth and shot off heavenward, taking the top half of her skull with it.

Guillaume and Guillemette, the fraternal twins, lay side by side in the soil, a pungent steam wafting upwards from the glistening contents of their gaping stomach wounds and mutilated bodies. They had lobbied hard to join the expedition. As Youths, they'd wished to see the world beyond the cassava farms of their home in Ardwood. Now they would never see anything again.

The dull palette of the mountain pass was now awash in shockingly vivid bursts of red, black, and brown. The distinctive aromas and curious sounds of the high-altitude flora and fauna had been replaced by the scent of fear and the echoing cries of the dying and dismembered.

Orianne began desperately seeking shelter. As she crawled through the melee, nausea and dizziness overwhelmed her senses. A gruesome assortment of desecrated anatomy were being tossed over her head, disappearing down the far side of the cliff face. She sunk lower, pressing her nauseated belly to the mud.

She slithered past dozens of disembodied legs, eyes, and tongues. Fragments of tooth and bone speckled the soil like stars against the night sky. She continued dragging herself along, being careful to avoid the ignited ends of the abandoned assegai. The blazing staves sizzled impotently as they scorched the ground.

She made it to the lower bend in the path where the expedition had established camp the night before, hoping to find refuge from the cold mountain air beneath the cluster of fallen Bulari trees. The opening had partially collapsed, but there was still enough space between the twisted branches for her to crawl through. She'd just made it to the opening when the ground beneath her chest shuddered. She turned her head and cast her gaze upon heresy made flesh.

Every muscle in her body froze. The hairs on her arms and neck stood at attention. Tears of dismay welled in her eyes. This wasn't just another farfadet. This was the Doyenne, the nightmarish leader of the hive.

The Doyenne tilted and jerked her head methodically, surveying the areas around Orianne. A pair of secondary eyes sat beneath both her left and right primary eyes. The sextet of unnervingly dispassionate, undoubtedly inhuman, sensory organs ensured that nothing could escape her gaze. All farfadet eyes lack irises, so in order to focus, they relied on constant head movements for visual acuity.

With her wings folded, her physique was human-like. Her draconic body, thick fibrous legs, and boney plates running down her spine and along the ridge of her prehensile tail whipping up the well-trodden soil with every thrash, immediately disproved any notions of humanity.

Orianne opened her mouth to scream, but the aural representation of her fears failed to complete the reflexive journey between the pit of her stomach and the top of her throat. She peered over her shoulder cautiously, slowly raising her eyes to the Doyenne's face.

Orianne steadied her thoughts. She inhaled deeply and thought back to what Asanda said moments before her horrific death. if these were to be the last moments drawing breath, Orianne didn't want to waste them on fear.

A sharp pain burst across her chest, pulsing outward from the old wound she'd acquired during Tutelage. Orianne instinctively gasped, but held her mouth to silence her yelping. It wasn't an internal ailment, so thankfully she wasn't succumbing to the Visitant pox. She worried she'd been struck by a venomous talon, but Orianne noticed that the Doyenne hadn't moved, and since farfadets weren't able to throw their talons the way carcolh snails could throw their quills, it must have been something else.

The Doyenne unleashed a blood-freezing cry. Orianne flattened herself against the mud. Her chest was on fire. The excruciating torment forced streams of tears from her eyes, but still she stayed prone.

The Doyenne raised her wings and pushed off, blowing a gust of cold wind and warm mud across Orianne's face, as she took to the still-darkened skies. By the time Orianne opened her eyes, the Doyenne was gone, soaring off into the distance with the rest of the hive.

Orianne crawled to her knees, held her aching chest and looked around. The expedition had been completely annihilated. The only noise was the diminishing sound of hundreds of leathery wings flapping off into the distance.

The pain in her chest subsided. Resting her forehead on the ground, Orianne wondered what could've caused such an intense, yet fleeting sensation.

Perhaps it was a bout of overwhelming panic festering deep within her consciousness spilling out across her flesh, merely a psychological reaction presenting as a physical affliction as a result of the situation. Whatever it was, she was fine now. She could move again.

Rubbing her chest, Orianne darted through the partially obscured opening in the cluster of fallen Bulari trees. After crawling through, she gathered sticks and large branches to block the opening from the inside. She wriggled toward the center of the makeshift hideaway and held her breath.

After a few harrowing moments of hearing nothing besides the thumping of her own heart, she collapsed into the dirt, sobbing unrepentantly. Although she'd spent many hundreds of nights memorizing field guides and tirelessly examining the academic texts during her Tutelage, the detailed accounts and graphically unabridged depictions of past expeditions had not prepared her for the relentless brutality she'd just witnessed first-hand.

She calmed herself and took stock of her current predicament. She was alone in the mountains of Ayrsulth. She had neither travelling supplies nor food. Even if she'd had food and supplies. There was no way to make the journey down the mountain before the temperature plummeted and the truly lethal winds began to blow.

Even if she survived the inhospitable elements, and the piercing sleet and blinding frost didn't kill her, there were any number of beasts and creatures- some even worse than farfadets- that would.

Orianne was well-versed in the history of her people. Across thousands of generations, throughout the entire history of Javari, only one person, Yvonne Lorraine, had ever successfully traversed the mountains during the Time of Verglas, but that storied account was questionable at best, closer to ancient fable than historical fact. Even if the incredible feats of Yvonne were true, that was millions of nights ago, when due to harsh necessity of the era, the people of Javari were much more biologically resilient .

"Orianne." a raspy voice called out.

Orianne jumped to her feet, banging her head on a thick low-hanging branch. As the world blurred in front of her, she could almost make out a shape in the darkness before her consciousness wafted away.

-TUTELAGE LESSON: FARFADETS-

Farfadets are indigenous to the Javari supercontinent, native to the hostile environments of Ayrsulth in region of Terre d'Os. It is believed that farfadets share a common ancestor to the now-extinct Kongamato, who during the time of the Progenitors, populated the same ecosystem. Farfadets live together in social groups called swarms.

Before the arrival of the Progenitors, Farfadet swarms covered all of Javari, though now, the entire species make their homes only in the treacherous mountains of Ayrsulth, in elaborate network of caves and tunnels called hives. The average swarm consists of around two dozen farfadets, though there have been reports of larger swarms exceeding two and even three hundred, with hives covering an area that would take more than three nights to traverse on foot.

Farfadets are divided into two tiers: the Sistren and the Doyenne. The majority of farfadets belong to the Sistren, with an estimated ratio of seventy-five to one hundred and fifty Sistren to each one Doyenne. The Farfadet social system is strictly adhered to and determined by nature rather than physical or political interactions amongst the members of the hive. The Sistren are roughly the size of a Javari Youth, while the rarely seen Doyenne, is a massive humanoid creature, standing taller than the largest Skinners and Searchers from Tolerbella. Sistren farfadets are also believed to lack the necessary anatomy and organs for reproduction, making the species dependent upon the Doyenne for continuation.

It is believed that Sistren farfadets produce the miraculous elixir known as coppermilk, which is the most valuable resource in all of Javari. Coppermilk possesses unparalleled healing and restorative properties. Sistren farfadets also guard the hives and protect the Doyenne. The exact nature of this process is unknown, however through cautious observation, it is believed that Sistren farfadets gather a nectar from special (as yet unknown) plants that only grown near the peaks of Ayrsulth and bring it back to the hives where the nectar is dehydrated, refined, and stored, turning it into coppermilk. Fetching coppermilk combs is the most dangerous, and most necessary task of the Vaincre and Explorateur stratum. Though in recent nights, combs have become rarer.

What little we know of the farfadets was obtained and provided by the accounts of the Wayfarer, Sha'del Mangati, of the Explorateur Stratum. Shortly after the defeat of the Visitants and Magyc creatures during the War of Progenitors, but before their final exile to Terre d'Os, Sha'del spent hundreds of nights among the farfadets, observing their behaviors.

-3-

Kyrian Le Rasoir checked his hastily scrawled map then turned his attention back to the road. They should reach The Filet Noir before the sky turned dark. He whistled a melancholy tune as he guided his cart through the rocky foothills on the border between Ayrsulth and Umadyn.

The somber melody he whistled kept Brie and Burgundy calm. The twin albino zebras pulling his cart could be temperamental on tranquil paths. On a desolate road where you were just as likely to see cute nest of swallows as you were to be attacked by bandits, keeping Brie and Burgundy relaxed was a necessity.

The winding path sat in a rugged basin nestled between two mountain ranges at the edge of the border between Terre de Sang and Terre d'Os. Curling ribbons of clouds obscured the peaks, but allowed some light to trickle through, and cast a lustrous sheen on the drab foliage.

Kyrian looked back over his shoulder at Marie, the "one-woman plague." She rolled her eyes and spat. Kyrian chuckled and returned his gaze to the path ahead. As they passed a marula tree, she plucked fruit from a branch and threw it. As it bounced off Kyrian's broad shoulders, he turned and stuck his tongue out. Marie smirked, Kyrian crossed his eyes, then they both broke into a fit of laughter.

Marie was neither a romantic nor familial companion. Their relationship was one of mutual respect and self-preservation. For a woman like Marie, small in frame with delicate features, having Kyrian at her side granted her a level of fear and respect among the lower, darker rungs of society. Her unparalleled wit and cunning was undoubtedly formidable, but the deplorable malevolents with whom they conducted their more unsavory affairs, weren't often swayed, or impressed by intellectual capacity.

For Kyrian, Marie's presence wiped away much of the corrosion from his heavily tarnished reputation. Her striking appearance and unflappable temperament lent an air of sophisticated credibility to the fearsome brute. They weren't particularly enamored of each other, but both recognized the undeniably mutualistic value of their collaboration.

"How much longer?" Marie asked with an exaggerated yawn, interrupting Kyrian's somber whistling.

"We should arrive before nightfall." Kyrian responded.

"I'm so bored." Marie sighed, "Remind me again, why we agreed to meet so close to the border of Terre d'Os?"

"Because by taking bigger risks, we'll be able to reap larger rewards." Kyrian retorted, casting a look over his shoulder at Marie, "Neither of us were content chasing goat thieves and adulterers along the eastern coasts."

"Truth." Marie conceded, "I just didn't realize that we would have to go so far."

"Dangerous people tend to reside in dangerous places." Kyrian shrugged.

"Why don't you tell me a story to pass the time." Marie asked, yawning.

"What do you want to hear?" Kyrian replied as Marie carefully moved from the back of the cart, climbing over the railing, and taking a seat next to him.

"How about something with trickery and bloodshed?" Marie smiled, "Something to set the mood for our upcoming rendezvous at Filet Noir."

"Trickery and bloodshed?" Kyrian thought for a moment, "Have I told you the fable of Vadim?"

"A fable?" Marie's smile faded, "I'm not sure a morality tale will spark my bloodlust."

"This one might." Kyrian smirked confidently. He reclined back in the wooden seat, and began the story…

Many generations ago, there was a beautiful man named Vadim Anaheb. Vadim possessed a brilliant mind, however, everyone he encountered was thoroughly enchanted by his beauty. It was more than a pleasing face. His appearance was grand, but he also possessed a natural gift for connecting with people.

Vadim dreamed of becoming a Skinner. He wanted to be seen as courageous and tough, not compassionate- and definitely not beautiful. So, during the Ritual of Avenir, Vadim declared his intent to join the Vaincre. But the Mentors placed him with the Unir Stratum. He travelled to Courbonne and after much convincing, was able to gain an audience with the Gold Chieftain, though his meeting was limited to three questions.

For his first question, Vadim asked to join the Vaincre, and was denied. For his second question, he asked to serve the Queenmothers of Tolerbella. That would allow him to remain in close proximity to the leadership of the Vaincre, while still serving the Unir. The Gold Chieftain denied him again. With one question left, Vadim realized he'd have to change his approach. For his final question, he asked for an ear of corn.

"An ear of corn?" Marie exclaimed.

"Yes. A single ear of corn." Kyrian continued…

Vadim knew that the Chieftain needed servants to tend to the needs of the Elders and other matters of Courbonne. So, Vadim asked if he could take the ear of corn and return a few nights later with one hundred servants, then would he be allowed to join the Vaincre? The Chieftain wasn't immune to Vadim's charms, and was in fact in need of servants, so he agreed to the terms, and gave Vadim a single ear of corn.

Vadim wrapped the ear of corn in fine ribbon and set off. After a couple of nights, he came across a village. He told the Village Elder that he was on a mission to deliver a special ear of corn to the Chieftain and requested a place to sleep for the night. The Village Elder agreed, and treated Vadim as an honored guest.

During the night, while all the villagers were asleep, Vadim fed the ear of corn to the Village Elder's chickens, leaving the fine ribbon in the coop.

The next morning, Vadim accused the Village Elder of being negligent in the care of his chickens. The Village Elder begged him to take ten chickens as an apology. Vadim accepted, then collected his ribbon and the chickens, and set off.

Vadim arrived at another village. Before he entered, he wrapped the ribbon around one of the chickens' necks.

He told the village Queenmother he was on a mission for the Chieftain and requested a place to store his special chickens for the night. Just like the first village, Vadim was treated as an honored guest.

During the night, Vadim butchered the chickens and smeared their blood and feathers on the door of the Queenmother's house, leaving the ribbon on the step. The next morning, he accused the Queenmother of slaughtering the chickens, and threatened to bring the wrath of the Chieftain down upon the village. The Queenmother begged Vadim to take fifty tri-horn goats as an apology. Vadim accepted, collected his ribbon and the tri-horn goats, and set off.

Vadim drove the tri-horn goats down the road. After a while, he came to a group of old men carrying a corpse. He asked them whose body they were carrying, and they replied that they'd found it on the shore and were taking it inland for burial.

Vadim offered to complete the burial if they would take his goats. The old men happily accepted the offer. As the old men counted the goats, Vadim withdrew his dagger and sliced their throats, spilling their dark blood on his cloak. Vadim covered the corpse in the old men's clothes and carried it on his back. Soon, he reached the beaches between Courbonne and Navanca.

Arriving at the port city, he told the Dominie that the person he was carrying was none other than Bashar Ahmad Jalal, the estranged, yet still beloved, first cousin of the Chieftain. Vadim said Bashar had been badly injured, but with rest, would make a recovery.

Vadim gripped his bloody cloak and told the Dominie that they had been attacked by Visitant marauders. Vadim requested a place to rest, and like the previous villages, Vadim was treated as an honored guest.

Late at night, Vadim snuck into the regal chambers and stole one of the Dominie's bejeweled bracelets. When morning came, Vadim asked the people to help him wake Bashar. The villagers beat drums, and banged on pots, but Bashar would not awaken.

Vadim tore away the ribbon revealing the face of the corpse who was undeniably dead. From the bedside, he presented the Dominie's bracelet, and accused the Dominie of murder.

The villagers seized the Dominie, bound him in irons, and dashed him against the jagged rocks along the coast of the Estuary. They begged Vadim to return to Courbonne and plead to the Chieftain for mercy.

Vadim agreed on the condition that they offer up one hundred of their best Youths to serve the Chieftain as penance for the Dominie's heinous crime.

They eagerly agreed to those terms, and fetched the strongest, most accomplished Youths, and presented them to Vadim.

Vadim returned to Courbonne and presented the youths to the Gold Chieftain. The Chieftain was so impressed, he granted Vadim's request to join the Vaincre, and offered Vadim the title of Skinner.

But Vadim declined. He realized that his ability to turn a single ear of corn into one hundred servants was irrefutable proof that he was a natural gifted politician. His talents would undeniably be best utilized right there in Courbonne, with the Unir Stratum…

"Wow!" Marie exclaimed, "That was truly an engaging tale of deception and bloodshed."

"I thought you might enjoy it." Kyrian nodded, "Were you able to spot the double deception?"

"The double deception?" Marie cocked her head.

"While Vadim tricked numerous people," Kyrian explained, "But he was deceived himself."

"By whom?" Marie asked scratching her head.

"The Gold Chieftain." Kyrian smiled, "For he was not only able to trick Vadim into ultimately joining the Unir Stratum, but he did so in a way that convinced Vadim to want to join of his own accord."

"That's fantastic!" Marie clapped with excitement, "Perhaps we too shall have an opportunity to compel our clients to willingly act in our own best interests."

"Perhaps." Kyrian nodded, "We are here."

Just ahead in the middle of an unnaturally made clearing in the woods, sat The Filet Noir. The desolate two-story tavern certainly lived up to its reputation as the refuge of the forgotten. Built with river stones and mudbricks, the outer walls were covered in lustrous dyes of red and black, but most of the paint had eroded away many generations ago.

The roof was curved and covered with grey tiles. The second floor was built asymmetrically, and slightly smaller than the first. Part of it hung over the edge of the floor below, creating a treacherous overhang on one side, and an equally precarious balcony on the other.

A signpost at the edge of the clearing warned travelers of the two rules one must abide went entering The Filet Noir. The first rule was "*Keep Yourself to Yourself.*"

Nobody came to The Filet Noir in search of camaraderie or general rapport with strangers, nor would anyone so foolish as to go looking for friendship, find it here.

The second rule etched into the knotty wood of the sign read: "*Ne Fais Pas,*" which means "do not do." As in, do not do anything that would capture the attention of, or bring attention to, the other patrons.

Kyrian stopped the cart near the overhanging side and tied Brie and Burgundy's reins to a stump. Marie jumped down off the cart and pulled back her traveling cloak. She adjusted the loops on her baldric, ensuring that the rows of throwing daggers strapped to it were secure in their sheaths.

Kyrian walked around to the back of the cart and withdrew his throwing clubs. The batons were long and smooth, with a 3-inch diameter knob of blackstone at the ends. He tucked them into his belt and adjusted his cloak so that his devastating weapons were hidden from view. They nodded to each other and headed to the entrance.

They pushed open the thick wooden doors. Like many taverns so far from more heavily populated areas, it lacked all but the most necessary of conveniences. A rush of air wafted over Kyrian and Marie. They were immediately overwhelmed by a host of offensive odors.

Stone columns supported the upper floor. The walls were covered in portraits and warning scrolls, all related to the nearby mountains. Above the massive bar, hung the freshly killed corpses of a trio of prairie boars.

The boars had been sliced open from throat to groin, and the blood from their wounds dripped down into a wooded trough that fed into a series of barrels. Most of the crimson fluid missed the trough, and pooled into dark, repulsive puddles on the ground beneath.

Kyrian and Marie looked at each other with a slight scowl. They weren't the types of people to be put off by disgusting sights and smells, but hundreds of nights spent in the more sophisticated surroundings of cities and large towns had made them somewhat discerning. It wasn't the unsanitary conditions of the bar, nor the repugnant aura of the patrons that put them off. It was what the state of the establishment represented. Places like this weren't the sort to attract those with means to pay handsome rewards.

Ignoring the anonymous patrons sitting at the shadowy tables lining the walls of the room, they approached the bar. Marie and Kyrian each pulled back a stool, but finding the seats moist and sticky, wisely opted to stand and lean instead. The bartender came out from behind the curtain and glared at the pair of mismatched newcomers.

His height was startling. The top of his thick, gray hair nearly brushed the hooves of the dangling dead boars. His face was angular, and just as asymmetrical as the building in which he made his living. His body had been disfigured by a lifetime of untreated wounds and neglected infections.

"Bienvenue." the bartender growled, eyeing them with a look that was equal parts disdain and distrust, "If you have any issues, settle them. Do you seek food, companionship, employment…perhaps all three?"

"Just food." Marie spat back, "We're not staying long."

"As long as you pay, we have no quarrel." the bartender sniffed, "Viande et riz. We have meat and rice."

"Good." Marie added, "And bring us some fermented milk to drink as well."

"Trente-huit." the bartender spat on the floor, "The price is thirty-eight shells."

"Only thirty-eight?" Marie pulled coins from her hip satchel and laid them on the bar, "We can do that."

"Trop d'argent. That's too much." The bartender counted the shells, "This is fifty. C'est cinquante!"

"Let's call it insurance." Marie arched an eyebrow.

"Quoi?" the bartender belched, "Insurance for what?"

"That the meat and milk are unspoiled." Marie smirked, "That we won't go running to a latrine right after eating."

The bartender stared at Marie. Marie stared right back. Kyrian kept an eye on the other patrons. Marie had deliberately mentioned their wealth loud enough for any to hear, but the buzz of the room remained a dull murmur. Suddenly, the bartender laughed, his voice resonating around the room like wet thunder.

"I like you, small woman." he chuckled scooping up the shells in his meaty palms and pulled a calabash from beneath the bar, "Je n'aime personne. I don't like anyone. But I like you. Take your drink. Find a table. Le bien?"

"Bien." Marie nodded, "Thanks."

Marie and Kyrian found a table and took a seat. Just as they'd opened the calabash, a decrepit looking woman burst through the doors followed by a half-dozen men clad in mismatched armor. Her ragged cloak dragged behind her soaking in all manner of repulsive and mysterious fluids as she made her way through the room.

The cloaked woman climbed onto a stool, reached within her cloak, and slammed the freshly decapitated head of a young child on the bar. The other patrons stood from their tables and cheered as she raised her veiny, wrinkled arms above her head and pulled down her hood.

"Are they really cheering because she killed a child?" Kyrian whispered between swigs.

"Apparently." Marie whispered back uneasily, "Let's hope Lanos arrives soon, so we can get out of this place."

"I bet the bartender is Lanos." Kyrian sighed.

"That ugly giant?" Marie laughed perplexed, I thought Lanos was referred to you by the man from Courbonne? Hard to imagine him keeping such company."

The cloaked woman banged on the bar. The bartender emerged from behind the curtain, displaying an annoyed look. When the cloaked woman saw his expression, she laughed it off. She threw off her hood, wrapped her sickly arms around his neck and planted a sticky, sloppy kiss in the center of his forehead.

"Why so sour? We've slain the picot!" the cloaked woman proclaimed, sparking another round of raucous applause from her men and the other patrons.

"Did that Visitant woman say picot?" Marie whispered.

"I believe so." Kyrian whispered back.

"I thought they were myths." Marie stared at the table but threw inconspicuous glances at the celebrating group.

"Not myths. Just rare." Kyrian took another sip, "Tall, birdlike, but without feathers or wings. They cover themselves in a weave of leaves, branches, and dung, then they wait by desolate paths, mimicking the wails of a child. When a curious traveler gets close enough, the picot slashes them open with its hooked beak, before pecking out their eyes and brains. It's a deceptive, yet effective predator."

"But that," Marie quipped, pointing, "is not the head of a bird-like creature on the bar. There is no beak. There are no talons or fangs. That is a child's head. And it looks like a *young* child's head at that."

"Indeed." Kyrian nodded, "Some believe if you survive an attack by a picot, but the wound doesn't heal properly, then your future children are born picots."

"Is that true?" Marie wrinkled her nose in disgust.

"Does it matter?" Kyrian shrugged "Visitants do not lend themselves to reason."

The conversation between the Visitant woman and the bartender began growing in intensity. Marie and Kyrian watched as the Visitant woman's jovial expression melted into a mask of annoyance and anger. With a piercing scream, the Visitant woman pushed the bartender back with surprising force. She nodded to her armor-clad entourage and headed towards the table where Kyrian and Marie sat.

"This won't be good." Kyrian muttered to Marie. Wiping his mouth, he stealthily slid his hands under the table to grip his throwing batons.

The Visitant woman and her entourage loomed over Kyrian and Marie. A cloud of rage darkened her already unsightly features. Her entourage pointed their blades at Kyrian as she angrily slammed her fist on the table and tilted her head toward the calabash.

"That's the last of the fermented milk!" she barked, slamming her fist on the table again, "Me and my champions are thirsty."

"That is unfortunate." Marie replied, "Quenching thirst is extremely important- especially in the cold, dry air of the mountains. Perhaps you all should take turns spitting in each other's mouths."

"FOOLISH SPRITE!" the Visitant woman's eyes bulged as she reached across and slapped Marie across the cheek, "DO YOU KNOW WHO I AM?!?!"

"I'm afraid I don't." Marie shook her head mockingly.

"Oh yeah, sprite?" the Visitant woman grinned smugly, licking her lips as she reached for the calabash, "Before my champions slice open your throat, know that you are in the presence of Cedonia Barkridge, the Blood Spouse of Azrael the Immolator, Second Herald of the Vanquishing Great, and Angel Queen of the Cedar Circle. I am known among Visitants and Javari alike. I am fire and pain and destruction and suffering---"

"And blind." Marie interrupted gravely.

"Blind?" Cedonia cackled, "You are a foolish sprite. As you can very well tell, there's nothing wrong with my vision. I can see you and your brute well enough."

"I'm afraid not, Cedonia Barkridge," Kyrian snarled, "you lost your vision in a bar fight."

Before Cedonia could comprehend the threat, Marie flicked her wrist. Two of her daggers flew from beneath the table, penetrating Cedonia's pupils with a sickening squelch.

As Cedonia howled in pain, Kyrian kicked over the table and lunged into the champion standing nearest to him. The champion's nose, skull, and teeth offered no resistance as they crumpled beneath the knob.

Two more of Cedonia's champions leapt into the fray. Marie swiftly opened their throats. A third champion grabbed Marie, only to be met with a dagger to the groin.

Kyrian ducked beneath the swing of a blade and smashed his assailant's knee, inverting the joint. Kicking over the howling champion, he stomped on his back, pulverizing the vertebrae, while repeatedly bashing him about the head, flattening it with his bloodied club.

Marie made quick work of another champion, shoving her dagger into his mouth while leaping over his shoulders, viciously dragging the blade up through his palate and sinuses, splitting the center of his face and forehead, the contents spilling out like watermelon pulp. Landing on her feet, she kicked Cedonia in the chest, sending the shrieking witch flying backwards into the bar.

The final champion looked at his fallen companions and ran for the door. Kyrian flung a baton, killing the terrified champion could make it across the gore-soaked threshold.

The patrons who'd been cheering when Cedonia first entered the tavern now jumped out of their seats. Pulling out a wide assortment of blades and clubs, they surrounded the pair, casting vulgar profanities and blasphemous threats. Kyrian and Marie exchanged bemused looks. They hadn't come for a fight but welcomed the chance for bloodshed.

The desperation of the patrons increased a hundred-fold. They weren't fighting for survival. They were trying to keep enough of their bodies intact so there would be something left for their kinsmen to bury.

Dozens of mortal coils weren't shed, so much as they were forcibly torn away. The tavern floor was clamor of the room fell quiet save for Kyrian and Marie's breathing, and the ear-shattering yowls of Cedonia, who trembled on the floor, clutching helplessly at the pair of serrated daggers embedded in her eyes.

Kyrian and Marie heard a loud rustle. The bartender emerged from behind the curtain, with a steaming platter.

"Tres impressionnat! I know now that your reputations weren't merely the work of fabrications or exaggerations. Demonstration is far more convincing than explanation." the bartender chuckled grimly.

Placing the food on the bar, he knelt down beside Cedonia and squeezed her head. She screeched as the bartender flattened her skull against his chest with a resounding crack of malevolent finality.

"This was all a set up?" Marie asked annoyed.

"Oui, small woman. It was not intended to be such, but when Cedonia and her champions arrived, I could not pass up the chance for a live demonstration of your skills." The bartender chuckled, brushing a few errant chunks of Cedonia's brain and skull fragments from his apron

"So that would make you…" Kyrian pointed.

"Je suis vraiment désolé. My apologies, but I had to be sure you were all that I've heard you to be." the bartender extended his hand warmly, "You are indeed Kyrian Le Rasoir. And you, small woman, you are none other than Marie, the one-woman plague. It is a pleasure to meet you. My name is Lanos Ndintu-Bel Acqwon, and I wish to commission your services."

"I knew it!" Kyrian smirked.

"You could have just asked for references." Marie spat, treading carefully to retrieve her daggers.

"Documents can be falsified." Lanos chuckled matter-of-factly, "Actions, however? Those cannot."

"You have a point." Marie conceded.

"For this particular task, I needed to be absolutely certain of your abilities." Lanos retrieved the platter of food from the bar and handed it to Kyrian.

"Fair enough." Kyrian chewed gluttonous mouthfuls of meat loudly, "But tell me, how did a man from Courbonne become the proprietor of this den of iniquity?"

"He's from Courbonne?" Marie exclaimed.

"Oui." Lanos smiled coyly.

"How can you tell?" Marie eyed Lanos suspiciously.

"His wounds are far too severe." Kyrian spoke knowingly, "And his height and strength? There is no training for such attributes. Lanos wields the Magycs."

"Indeed, Kyrian," Lanos smiled devilishly, "You are very observant. Buy you didn't come here for my biography, non? You came here for a task. And I have an extremely lucrative one to offer."

"Go on." Kyrian agreed.

"Some forty nights ago, a large Vaincre expedition headed up into the mountains." Lanos began, "But now Verglas is upon us."

"So, they're dead." Marie interrupted, knocking away another handful of meat from Kyrian's fist, "And those who aren't, we kill, and retrieve their supplies and weapons?"

"No." Lanos responded flatly, "I don't want their bodies or their war toys. I want something more valuable. Heading into Ayrsulth so near to the Time of Verglas means that they're seeking the Veil of Bone, and the source of coppermilk. Since they have not yet returned…"

"Then they must've been successful in their quest to find the coppermilk source!" Marie exclaimed.

"Precisely." Lanos nodded, "If they are alive, then it's because they've found coppermilk. If they are not alive, they still were on the right track. I'd like you to trace their path, find and kill whatever is left of the expedition, and draw me a route to the source. I will give you five hundred thousand shells now, another two-hundred and fifty thousand when you return, and as much coppermilk as you can carry."

Lanos waved his scarred, boiled-covered arm. Two canvas sacks appeared in front of him. Each sack was overstuffed, filled to the brim with shells. Marie gasped and put her daggers away. Her eyes went wide as she dug her hands into the smooth, oval coins.

Kyrian was much better at masking his astonishment, focusing instead on something even more valuable than the wealth newly manifested in front of him, information. He noticed that Lanos' arm had fresh scars. Those from Courbonne were encouraged to master the necessary skills to bend Magycs to their will, but one can only bend something so far, before it inevitably breaks.

Lanos noticed Kyrian peering at his wounds, and quickly disappeared through the curtain behind the bar.

"Marie," Kyrian whispered, "Did you notice Lanos' arm? It seemed that the Magycs disagree with him. He is beginning to rot from overuse."

"So long as he pays the reward before he loses the ability to conjure more, then let him rot." Marie whispered back, dredging up fistfuls of coins, and letting them rain down between her hands, back into the sacks.

"No," Kyrian chewed the last of the meat, "If he tries to deceive us, we have an advantage."

"Excellent." Marie nodded, "But not before he pays."

"So," Lanos proclaimed, returning through the curtain with a towel covering his wounded arm, "We have come to an arrangement, oui?"

"Agreed." Marie smiled greedily.

"Excellent." Lanos agreed, "Feel free to take whatever you need from these corpses you created. Fill your cart with some provisions from my kitchen. But you must leave at once, they have a forty-night head start."

-4-

Orianne woke up screaming. The blanket felt soft against her skin but was heavy from her sweat. She didn't know how she arrived here, but the warm light streaming through the window above the mat made it clear that she was no longer on the mountain path. Somehow, she'd been moved to a recovery hall.

A few bowls containing peaches, honey-glazed dates, and spicy rice sat on the small bedside table. A small placard leaned against a tiny cup of coppermilk. The penmanship on the placard was exquisite:

"Javari. Terre de Sang. Chest and arm wounds. 38 nights."

The number disturbed her. How could it possibly have been thirty-eight nights? And what was that about her chest wound? That had been healed long before she joined the expedition.

She sat up and greedily empty the bowls of their contents, saving the coppermilk for last. The medicinal properties were enhanced when you drink it with a full belly, and it slid down Orianne's throat like silk, and warmed her body like heat from a hearth. Fully revived, she stood, stretched, and tried to get her bearings. Looking around the hall she allowed herself a moment to lose herself in the incredible artistry of the design.

Lustrous braziers on polished stilts sat at the base of ornate support columns, providing ample light and comfortable heat in the cavernous hall. An octet of enormous bronze and ivory statues depicting elders and ancestors encircled the ceiling, looking down on Orianne with permanently frozen stares. A large, plush orchid rug split the room down the center, running the entire length of the hall, from the sets of intricately carved doors at the far end, all the way to a row of Observer thrones, just a few mats down from where she stood.

She ran her fingers along the arm of one of the Observer thrones. It was carved from the trunk of a baobab tree and adorned with kudu hide pillows. Fixed on each of the broad feet were ivory boxes containing parchment and quills, so the Observers and attending Patricians could take their notes. She froze, realizing the décor was that of Citadelle de Carteaux, the Navancan recovery hall.

Stumbling back, the walls around her began to melt. The elegant décor crumbled and disintegrated. The lustrous braziers and onyx support columns buckled and warped. Everything in her line of sight began to decay and rot. She crawled on the floor, dragging herself away from the bewildering putrefaction of the room.

She reached the heavy doors at the end of the hall and pushed, but the pleasing curves of the wood carvings turned sharp and faded to a dull grey. The light vanished and the temperature dropped. Her eyes widened as she found herself in the midst of a damp and suffocating darkness.

"Do not be afraid, Orianne Duchamp." a raspy voice rang out beside her. Whipping her head around, she was face to face with the dispassionate eyes of the Doyenne!

"You can speak!" Orianne cried. It was less a question than a startled declaration of disbelief.

"No." the Doyenne replied calmly, "You hear me in your tongue, because your mind interprets it as such."

"How am I here?" Orianne tried to steady her nerves and hold back the wave of fear flooding her being, but the cracking pitch of her voice betrayed her true emotions.

"Do not be afraid." the Doyenne's voice was no longer raspy, but dulcet, "I had this chamber prepared, so you could recover from your wounds."

"My wounds?" Orianne's nerves began to settle.

"Yes. You lost consciousness on the mountain. You would have succumbed to the cold had I not brought you here and allowed your mind to create a place of comfort so your body could mend."

"I remember hitting my head…after escaping the battle. Orianne began, "Your farfadets killed the entire expedition. You were about to kill me!"

"One so frail should not be so presumptuous." the Doyenne seemed to chuckle, "If I wanted your life, I would have easily taken it."

"Then why didn't you?" Orianne retorted, more contentiously than she'd intended, "Why was I spared?"

"You did not intend to harm us, so why should I have harmed you?" The pragmatism of the Doyenne's tone caught Orianne off guard.

"I serve the expedition. I would've killed if I had to."

"I am in your mind. One should not speak falsely when their thoughts so readily betray their words."

"I was…" Orianne conceded, "I was following the instructions I was given."

"You were trying to get the others to turn back."

"Yes." Orianne confessed, "I saw the early signs of Verglas and was trying to turn them back. My role was one of consultation and expertise. I was there to assist and protect, not kill and destroy."

"Indeed. Your people sought to find our home and take our nutrients and resources. They sought to murder my Sistren and children, to annihilate my race. You sought only to keep breath in bodies. That is why you are here while your fellow warriors lie in the forever sleep."

"You misunderstand." Orianne pleaded, "We were only seeking to find help for our people."

"Tell me, is it customary for your kind to seek assistance with weapons drawn? To march on your neighbor with swords and spears? To eradicate those you beg for help? If so, I'm curious as to how you declare war."

"You must forgive our ignorance." Orianne felt foolish in the face of the Doyenne's irrefutable rationale, "We were seeking coppermilk. We only brought protection to defend against those that would do us harm."

"Do *you* harm?" the Doyenne's voice remained calm, but contained incredulous undertones, "I did not send our warriors and spies to your lands, to take your sustenance, leaving nothing in return. Invaders fearing the invaded? The same fears your leaders have cast upon us are the same fears those you call Visitants once cast upon you."

"I don't understand." Orianne cried, "Visitants?"

"You are an Instructor, an educator." the Doyenne nodded, "Your purpose is to teach others, but have you forgotten what your predecessors taught you?"

A bright light glowed as a large Tutelage scroll formed in Orianne's hands. She looked down in astonishment. It was one of the accounts she'd written during Tutelage. It even contained her handwritten notes along the margins.

"We are in Ayrsulth, one of the twin regions of Terre d'Os, which is also known as the Land of Bones. Ayrsulth, is closer to our homelands, and more hospitable than Umadyn, the other region. Both regions are…"

"Go on." the Doyenne encouraged, "Keep reading."

"Both regions are as malicious as they are desolate. While many generations have successfully ventured deep into the dark lands, it has largely remained an untouched wilderness, home to all manner of beasts and monstrosities, yet still a vast landscape of endless potential. Between the labyrinthine depths of the Fleshwater Ocean to the North, and the jagged, unforgiving peaks of the Angelical Dunes in the South, Ayrsulth and Umadyn are twin worlds forged and folded by ferocity. Terre d'Os is unfit for our people. Indeed, it is unfit for all people. The inhabitants there are worthy of no consideration other than to serve as a threat against our prosperity and must be destroyed."

"You've read edited words," the Doyenne waved her arm, entrancing Orianne, "but to truly understand, you must see the truth of your history unabridged, free from the deliberate revisions of devious motive. "

-5-

In her entranced state, Orianne found herself transported. The voice of the Doyenne blew through her ears like the soft, warm winds of the planting season, narrating the scenes playing out before Orianne's eyes. Though the account was familiar, there was much more Orianne had never before heard or witnessed.

The gulf between determination and delirium is both infinite and invisible. The poetry of the damned often falls on deaf ears. The will of a people may echo for miles without answer. But faith can only be deemed folly in the hindsight of forfeit. Seven thousand generations ago, the Progenitors labored tirelessly to build a thriving civilization. The results of their onerous burden took root and spread to the furthest shores.

Through procreation and exploration, they blanketed the lush and fruitful continent. They named their world Javari, in tribute to Queen Chief Sauvanne Figuier Javari, the fallen matriarch who freed them from bondage, braved the endless depths of the Fleshwater Ocean, and led them through the unfathomable to set foot upon their new homelands.

Tens of thousands of nights passed as they matured and prospered, building a complex and relatively equitable society. For the first few hundred generations, they lived in benevolent harmony with the mystical indigenous creatures, all of whom were wonderous and beautifully necessary to the prosperity of the land, in their own distinctive ways.

The kongamato gave them meat and building materials. They learned what crops to eat, what fields to plow, and how to safely avoid the hazards of chacals and carcolhs. They learned to forge weapons and build ships. They mastered the strategies of conquest by studying the hunting tactics of the gbahali, and migration patterns of the leviathans.

But it was my kind, the farfadets who guided them in the ways of immingling with the space between the miraculous and the mundane and develop the necessary skills to wield the preternatural abilities of the Magycs.

Then the Visitants arrived. They came from across the oceans, travelling some ninety-one nights, they sought to empower themselves in the name of their cursed homelands. The lands from which they came possessed a few natural resources, but nowhere near the abundant array of plants and animals, of fine minerals and raw materials. They were also wholly devoid of preternatural knowledge and had no comprehension in the true power of the Magycs.

The Visitants carried with them strange armaments and advanced technologies, but their deadliest weapon was unseen to the Progenitors. There was a pox in their blood. One for which there was no remedy, and one that threatened to decimate not only the stricken Visitants, but all life on Javari.

The Bronze, Iron, and Gold chieftains, the hall of elders, along with the Queenmothers and Mentors from all the regions, along with the beings from Ayrsulth, gathered to discuss the Visitant issue. They didn't want to let them die, but at the same time, could not endanger their own peoples. They decided that the Visitants, with their frail biology, ignorance of the natural ways, and crippling foreign sickness, could stay in the coastal region along the Southern border of Courbonne, just a few nights journey north of Navanca. The Visitants agreed, thankful for the merciful generosity of the Javari people.

At first, the arrangement worked. The Visitants stayed in their area, receiving instructions on how to work the land, grow food, and build shelter. Emissaries from their enclave were allowed to travel to other regions to learn necessary skills. But the emissaries would return to their enclaves, with stories of the splendor of the other regions, and after two generations, the Visitants became covetous. They gazed upon the magnificent people of Tolerbella, Ardwood, Navanca, and Courbonne, and devised plans to conquer the continent.

The Visitants sent word back to their homelands, and over the next few hundred nights, thousands of Visitants began arriving. This time they bore astonishing weapons of war and exotic beasts of battle. They attempted to take the organic riches of Javari for themselves, planning to extend their invasive empire, enslave and exterminate the people, and exploit the abilities of the magical beings.

The Progenitors partnered with the magical creatures and defeated the Visitant forces. The survivors were exiled to a narrow band of land between Terre d'Os and Terre de Sang. It was far from the coastal waters, and regularly beset upon by picots and carcolhs. Even when the monsters were held at bay, the terrain itself was suitable for little more than basic survival and necessary sustenance, but the alternative was death.

The exiled departed swiftly, and without protests. In the aftermath, the peace between the regions began to crack. The people of Ardwood were resentful of those from Tolerbella for damaging their lands in the march to the coasts. Those in Navanca felt undervalued, for though they didn't have as many warriors to offer, they were instrumental in devising winning strategies. Those in Tolerbella thought that as the front-line fighters, they should be entitled to more of the spoils, and were extremely displeased with having the enemy they'd just spent a generation fighting, now comfortably settled just a few nights north of their borders.

Courbonne however, being closest to the initial Visitant enclave on the shores where the invaders arrived, suffered the most fatalities and casualties. They blamed the magical creatures for not doing enough to protect them. Wanting to make amends, the creatures of Ayrsulth began teaching Courbonne how to wield the Magycs in order to strengthen their people and repair the deep scarifications of war.

However, as Courbonne became more and more proficient in the mystical arts, their arrogance grew. They became convinced that they should be the rulers of all Javari. The only thing stopping them was the knowledge held by the creatures inhabiting the lands of Ayrsulth.

Courbonne sent their strongest defenders, and most skilled at wielding Magycs to launch a surprise attack. Within a dozen nights, the defenders from Courbonne slaughtered the thousands of great beasts, driving the kongamato and gbahali to extinction, and nearly wiping out the entire population of carcolh and farfadets.

The creatures fought valiantly but were overwhelmed and unprepared for the vicious onslaught. Nearing annihilation, they brokered a conditional peace. In exchange for an end to the bloodshed, they would banish themselves to the mountains, where the terrain and climate were unsuitable for people.

Courbonne agreed to the terms. They returned home and called a meeting of all the peoples of Tolerbella, Ardwood, and Navanca. They lied and said the creatures had grown fond of the Visitants, and attacked them, but the brave defenders of Courbonne were able to banish the traitorous beings and protect the people in all the regions of Javari.

Celebrated as heroes, the leaders of Courbonne then established the strict social hierarchy known as the Stratums, to maintain power and order. And this is the way it was and the way it continues to be, but a single truth still yet stands…

…whatever has begun, can also be undone.

Orianne burst into tears as the trance faded. She didn't mean to lose her composure, but while the words on the parchment may have been open to interpretation, what she had witnessed with her own eyes was far beyond authentic.

She recalled thousands of nights worth of studies and stories, being informed and enthralled by tales of the fearsome monsters from Terre d'Os, the Land of Bones. Thousands of nights of hearing the village, region, and Stratum leaders warn about the unknown dangers in the lands to the north. She hung her head in shame, the ignominy of the realization weighed down on her chest.

"Forgive my ignorance, Doyenne." Orianne begged quietly, "I was unaware."

"Doyenne?" the Doyenne's voice lilted in bemusement, "Why do you address me as such?"

"Is that not your designation?" Orianne wiped her eyes, "Are you not the Doyenne, the ruler of the farfadets?"

"How amusing!" the Doyenne cackled, "Are your kind truly so arrogant as to bestow a title upon a foreign culture without any knowledge of the culture in question?"

"I meant no offense."

"Of course you didn't." the Doyenne replied flatly, "In your tongue, I would be known as Kiyolowe. I am not a ruler. I am the leader of the last Sistren. That the distinction between the two is lost on you, says a lot."

"My apologies, Kiyolowe." Orianne bowed her head again, "I do not wish for my final moments to have been tainted by faux pas. Please allow me a moment to compose my words more carefully before my execution."

"Your execution?" Kiyolowe laughed, "Is your kind is so malevolent they cannot fathom a living creature being anything else. I have no intention of killing you."

"KIYOLOWE!" a hoarse cry blared out.

"You see this!" Kiyolowe screeched at Orianne, her six eyes blazing, "Even now, in the Time of Verglas, your kind still comes to threaten my home!"

"No, it can't be!" Orianne argued, "Everyone in the expedition was killed. Either by battle, or the pox. That group took hundreds of nights to coordinate. For another expedition to be formed so quickly is not possible!"

"It is of little matter!" Kiyolowe waved her arm. The air around her wrist began to ripple and twist like a whirlpool in a lagoon. The spiral of distortion grew until it was taller and wider than both of them. Kiyolowe placed her hand firmly on Orianne's back and pushed her through.

Orianne landed on the frozen mountain path. A thick glaze of black frost coated the grass and trees. The disembodied limbs of the expedition had become grotesque obelisks buried beneath a layer of permanent shadow.

Orianne immediately began searching for cover. The winds forced her eyes to water, the tears freezing the instant they spilled, leaving black streaks down her cheeks. A bright light caught her attention.

Squinting through the cold, the light grew brighter as she approached. It was a long spear with two black stripes and three white stripes on the hilt.

"My assegai!" she exclaimed.

Throwing back her cloak, she pulled out the weapon and held the ignited tip as close as she could without touching the dangerously incendiary surface, trying desperately to draw in as much heat as possible.

She noticed some shapes in the distance. She wiped her eyes and stared again. Tucking her assegai under her arm to keep the warmth of the ignited tip close to her body, she continued moving towards the shapes in the distance. They were human-like, but bulky. It was as though a dozen strikingly tall men were carrying satchels on their backs. Could it really be another expedition?

As she advanced further, the shapes stopped. In spite of the heat from her assegai, Orianne shivered. Not from the cold this time, but from the fear of realization. The shapes were much closer now, and it was clear that they weren't another expedition.

It was a pack of chacals.

-TUTELAGE LESSON: CHACALS-

Unlike other Magyc creatures, chacals are not naturally occurring. Their existence is solely attributed to the intentional desires of the wielder. During the time of the Progenitors, it was a fate reserved as punishment for the most atrocious malefactors.

At the time, there was a bit of controversy over sentencing a Javari citizen to be forever damned to live the rest of their lives in a feral, devolved state of purgatory trapped in the realm between dead man and living jackal. While the criminal deviants indeed deserved some manner of retribution, surely, even those who'd committed a horrific transgression should at the very least, be allowed to retain their humanity. The debate raged back and forth with both sides acknowledging the legitimacy and rationale of the opposing viewpoints, while passionately refusing to concede their positions.

It seemed that there was no definitive way to determine with finality, whether the act was brutally harsh but societally appropriate, or if the mystical condemnation stretched beyond the boundaries of judicious objectivity. It wasn't until the case of Aubin Blindgrove, that this issue was ultimately resolved.

As a Youth, Aubin showed immense potential. During his Tutelage, he regularly completed his trials and tasks with top marks. When he pledged Unir Stratum, the Mentors recommended he skip the introductory tier of Aristo and begin his tenure in Courbonne as a Patrician. Honored though he was, Aubin politely declined the accelerated promotion, noting that it would likely garner resentment among the members of the Stratum.

The Mentors praised his refusal, citing his acute foresight as more evidence of his sagacity. Even after his arrival in Courbonne, as he went about the lowly duties of an Aristo, the winds carried whispers of Aubin being in line for chieftain, perhaps even the youngest Javari in history to ascend to the seat of Elder.

The reason however that Aubin is not remembered as an Elder is because for all of his political brilliance, despite his notable intellect, he was preposterously thin-skinned. His ego was as fragile as a swallowtail butterfly. The slightest offense would send him into a frenzy.

One evening while serving refreshments at the midday luncheon of the Elders, Tamela Najafi caught his eye. She was the niece of the Iron Chief, who'd stopped in Courbonne on a brief holiday while accompanying a cartography expedition across the continent.

As an Aristo, he was not allowed to speak during the meeting, unless specifically instructed otherwise. He waited until Tamela excused herself and followed her into the hallway. She'd reached the end of the magnificent corridor before she noticed him. Mistaking his infatuation for a sense of tenacious duty, she politely asked him to return to his station in the dining hall.

Mildly saddened by her oblivious rejection, he began the long walk back, all the while devising plans for another encounter. As he got to the doorway, his friend Nilerea Tolous exited carrying a heavy brass tray with the empty plates stacked neatly atop.

Nilerea asked him what he was doing in the hall, and Aubin explained that he was in love. He'd been mesmerized by the endless beauty of Tamela and couldn't help himself. Though Aubin admitted that following her was somewhat foolish, he boasted that his feelings were such, that he would march into the dining hall and ask the Iron Chief for permission to romantically pursue her niece, if Tamela was so inclined.

Nilerea smiled empathetically at her smitten friend, and told him while his attraction may be overwhelming, he should hold his tongue. Aubin was still just an Aristo, Nilerea advised, it would be bad form to approach the Iron Chief so directly, especially during the midday luncheon. Aubin interpreted this as mockery and snatched the tray from Nilerea's hands.

The plates shattered against the stone floors, drawing the attention of the Elders, who ran out into the hallway to investigate the commotion disrupting their meeting. They bursts through the great doors and shrieked in horror at the scene before them. Aubin had taken the heavy brass tray and had battered and pummeled Nilerea's head into a crimson pulp of broken teeth and shattered skull fragments.

The Chiefsguard attempted to subdue him, but the still-enraged Aubin was relentless. He killed eight of them, while the Chiefs retreated back into the dining hall, and sent the other Aristos fleeing out of the windows and service doors to fetch reinforcements. By the time he was finally restrained, the pile of corpses blocked the hall. Aubin had brutally taken life from over two dozen Aristos and Chiefsguard.

When brought before the Elders to answer for his heinous act, the Gold Chieftain asked to speak to Aubin alone. She deduced that while intellectually, Aubin's wit was astonishing, his emotional maturity was that of a Youth who'd drawn breath for three-thousand nights.

Returning to the judgement chamber, the Gold Chieftain decreed that she would not vote for him to be transformed into a chacal and expelled from Terre de Sang, but instead recommended that he be imprisoned in Navanca, where the Instructors and Dominies could attempt to foster his interpersonal mind, so that it may one day match his academic brilliance.

Though the vote of the Bronze Chieftain counts tenfold, the unanimous, dissenting vote from the Iron and Gold Chieftains, and all of the Elders, overruled her. As Aubin was taken away to be prepped for his transformation, the Gold Chieftain made the following decree:

"As Gold Chieftain, I have a weighted influence on the outcome of a trial. The voice of our council has spoken, and I accept their decision. In terms of the laws that govern our great land however, all may speak, but I alone am heard. From this night forward, using the Magycs to condemn any and all within the borders of Javari to spend their final days of breath as a chacal is forbidden. Never again, shall we conflate justice with vengeance. When a cart has a broken wheel, we do not slaughter the oxen or burn the carriage. We patch, mend, and repair. As I have said it, so let it be so..."

.

-6-

Cossette Archambault walked down the ornate gangway of the Carronade. She loathed sea travel, and though the Carronade was more palace than ship, she preferred the rustic comforts of her country estates over the luscious appointments of the floating suites. As both Bronze Chieftain and the senior wife in the most affluent family in the region, she was no stranger to opulence. She was quite accustomed to unfathomable luxuries.

She didn't take her fortune for granted, and she appreciated that her husband Cassius gave her lavish gifts. She simply wished that the gifts he gave aligned with her interests. Commissioning the Carronade and sending her on a private holiday would've been a dream, but for someone who hated the ocean, it was a nightmare.

The ride from the coast was pleasant. No matter how annoyed Cossette was at sea travel, there was nothing she loved than the natural scenery of her home. The Princièrement District was a sprawling landscape of sweeping meadows, red sand beaches, and shimmering silver cliffs leading to Lavoi, the capitol city of Courbonne.

"Welcome home, sister." Gerald smiled extending his arms to help Cossette off the final step of the gangway, "Six thousand nights at sea is quite the holiday for one who hates boats. Tell me Cossette, how did you get through it?"

"Wine." Cossette smiled, ". After many dull nights, the captain mentioned that we were nearing l'Archipel Infini. I immediately made the crew dock, then I disembarked and spent the remainder of my time hunting, drinking, and singing songs to the cormorants."

"Well, you've returned at an interesting time, sister."

"Is that so?"

"Indeed." Gerald took her arm as they walked. "It seems that the esteemed Archambault family will be expecting an heir."

"Gerald," Cossette stopped walking, "It has been countless nights since any families of Courbonne have successfully delivered new life. If this your attempt at a joke, you'll need to try again. This one isn't funny."

"It's not a joke. Look." Gerald responded flatly. He pulled a small scroll from his purse and handed it to her. "It was announced just a few nights ago. Cassius' most favored mistress, Aurelia, is expected to give birth sometime within the next twenty-two nights."

Cossette read the parchment. Her face was as motionless as carved stone. Gerald wasn't joking. It was true. The family's first heir, the first child born in the region in a generation, wouldn't be produced by one of her husband's wives, but by his mistress.

"And he was elated by this news?" Cossette asked.

"Indeed. When he learned Aurelia was pregnant, he threw a feast for seventy nights."

"Seventy nights?" Cossette grimaced, still managing to mask her anger, "Do you remember the celebration feast after Cassius asked for my hand and I accepted?"

"I do." Gerald nodded, "It lasted three nights."

"Gerald." Cossette spoke calmly.

"Yes, sister?"

"Do you know where my husband is right now?"

"Shortly after your departure, he had left for the Villa for a meeting with the Elders to discuss the situation with the lack of coppermilk."

"That's unfortunate." Cossette's voice dropped.

"I do however know where Aurelia is right now." Gerald remarked casually, a knowing look in his eye, "She's in Ardwood, just at the border actually. Or rather she *was* in Ardwood prior to her tragic accident."

"Oh?" Cossette eyed Gerald carefully.

"My dear sister," Gerald began, "As you were away, I took the liberty to send some special attendants to express your feelings for the mother to be."

"Brother," Cossette whispered, "I definitely had some *feelings*. It's not often the wealthiest man in Courbonne sires a child with a woman who has drawn breath for only eight thousand nights. But you didn't?"

"Indeed, I did."

"I am his senior wife, and the Bronze Chieftain."

"And we share blood my sister," Gerald smiled deviously, "I'd thought you want to mark the occasion."

"But Gerald…"

"Aurelia is not dead. But the offending offspring is no longer a concern. Would you like me to have the servants prepare your elephant and howdah, so you may visit your husband, and deliver the tragic news personally?"

"No," Cossette shook her head, " If my attendants and I make journey to the Elders, there would be too much fanfare. You have placed me in a most awkward position. Send for a shellskin."

"I apologize, sister." Gerald bowed his head, "I was acting in the interests of the family."

"My dear brother," Cosette's voice was soft but grim, "it is not your family. And as such, any interests were not yours to act upon. This compulsive streak of yours? This lack of foresight? That is why you were passed over. That is why I sit as Bronze Chieftain."

"Yes, my sister." Gerald swallowed hard and exhaled slowly, "Shall I have the shellskin journey to Ardwood to finish the job?"

"No. That would arouse too much suspicion. Have them journey to the Villa instead."

"Do you mean?" Gerald was briefly taken aback.

"It's the only way." Cosette responded flatly, "If Aurelia were to die now, everyone, including my husband-especially my husband- would look to me as the culprit. But if my husband were to meet his end…"

"And you're certain a shellskin should handle this?"

"That's what they do, is it not?" Cossette frowned annoyed, "They trade skins for shells. I've got a lot of shells, so I desire a lot of skin. I need to journey to Tolerbella, see how the expeditions are progressing. While I am gone, send for a shellskin, and undo this mess."

"As you have said it, so let it be so." Gerald nodded.

Twelve nights later, a shellskin in heavy cloak arrived at the service entrance to the Archambault estate. He climbed down from his cart and handed the reins to the servants. Wiping the sweat from his eyes, he followed a group of attendants through the plantain orchards and rows of trade huts where the artisans smelted iron, weaved cloths, and assembled fine works of beaded jewelry.

As they turned down a winding path, the cloaked man stopped for a brief moment, to gaze in awe at the majesty of the legendary Archambault menagerie.

Stories of its splendor had been shared throughout Javari, but seeing it in person, he was genuinely taken aback by the exotic wonders. Horses, camels, and elephants chewed their feed lazily in the sables. Handlers worked with hunting hyenas and ostriches in the training pens. The chief veterinarian dissected the corpse of a freshly killed minke whale, lecturing to a wholly captivated audience of apprentices as she worked.

Finally, they reached a private walkway leading to the entrance of the main house. The attendants pulled open the large, reinforced doors, and motioned for Kyrian to enter. Stepping through, Kyrian found himself in a spacious vestibule that was larger than the home he grew up in.

"Welcome, shellskin. Please leave your belongings on the table." Gerald's voice rang out from behind the door.

"Are you sure?" the shellskin looked down at the thin marble top of the table, and its narrow, wooden legs, "My bags are heavy, and this table looks delicate."

"Please leave your things there." Gerald replied.

With a sigh, the shellskin removed his satchel and placed it gently. To his mild astonishment, the marble top didn't crack. The legs didn't buckle.

"I've placed them." the shellskin man called out.

"Good." Gerald responded, "You may enter."

The shellskin pulled the inner door open and stepped through the entryway into the longest room he'd ever seen. Magnificent glass windows sat high on the wall, neighbored by draperies colored in vibrant shades of purple, red, yellow, and green, the bottoms and ends of which were adorned with gold braided tassels and white sueded linings.

A plush rug, as blue-black as the sky during a maelstrom ran from the door through the center of the room splitting into two paths at the center. One path curved left towards a set of double doors, each as tall as a baobab tree. The other path swept gracefully to the right, leading to an imposing ivory throne perched beneath a massive portrait of the Courbonne landscape.

Gerald stood by the entrance and nodded. He was immediately impressed with the shellskin's demeanor. This one seemed to appreciate his surroundings.

Gerald politely allowed the shellskin to take it all in, before escorting him down the plush carpet leading to the throne. Gerald sank confidently into the cushions.

"Please," Gerald smiled, "Take a seat."

"Thank you, but I've been travelling many nights." the shellskin demurred, "I wouldn't want to soil your cushions."

Jumping to his feet, Gerald grabbed the edges of the thick cushion and pulled it from the throne. The pillow was as long as Gerald was tall, so it took a bit of effort to get it onto the floor. The shellskin raised his eyebrows in shock when Gerald pulled opened his robe and began urinating on the luxuriant cushion. When he finished defiling the seat. Gerald closed his robe and clapped his hands five times. Ten servants rushed through the double doors.

"Fetch me a new cushion." Gerald commanded, "And take this one to the Chief veterinarian. She can give it to the old stud bull to sleep on."

Without a word, six servants ran back through the double doors. The four remaining servants grabbed the corners of the stained cushioned and hurried out of the room through the small entry door. No sooner than the four had left, the other six returned with a brand-new cushion.

"I've seen a lot in my journeys." the shellskin took a seat next to Gerald on the fresh cushion.

"Have you?" Gerald leered.

"But I've never seen a man piss on a pillow."

"Demonstration far outweighs explanation." Gerald smirked, "Had I told you that your current state was of no concern, you would've thought I was just being polite. After what you've just seen, surely now there is no doubt?"

"Indeed." The shellskin nodded.

"Besides," Gerald smiled, "You may be built like a field ox fresh off the yolk, but your manner of speech and the condition of your garments are *mildly* impressive."

The shellskin looked down as his clothing. His agbada was a bit dusty, but free from tears or stains. The sleeves of the finely woven shirt fit snuggly against his muscular arms. The cuffs of his pants were frayed, but he'd remembered to tuck them into his boots before he arrived at the estate. He didn't look wealthy, but his overall appearance was far more polished than the average shellskin.

"With respect, Seigneur Gerald," the shellskin nodded, "I've traveled a dozen nights to honor this request, and I'm certain that you didn't call for my presence here today merely to discuss fashion."

"No, I did not." Gerald's tone flattened, "I have another task for you. One requiring discretion. One that serves the Archambault family."

"I have not one the tongue or temper for gossip." the shellskin nodded, "Though I must ask, if this task is for Archambault family, should we not wait until an Archambault is present?"

Gerald shifted in his seat. He kept the corners of his lips tight so as not to lose the smile on his face, but the light in his eyes dimmed ever so slightly. A clever shellskin was a good thing, but perhaps this one was *too* clever.

"My sister, the mistress of house, and the Bronze Chieftain of our land, is on holiday. But she has given me full liberty to tend to this matter."

"I see."

"Our beloved patriarch has committed a grave offense. Go to the Elders' Villa at the northern coast of Courbonne and take the breath from his body."

"You wish for me to dispose of your brother-in-law?" the shellskin stood and headed towards the entry door.

"Yes."

"The husband of the Bronze Chieftain?"

"Yes."

"And if I encounter any impediments from the Elders? Am I to dispatch with them as well?"

"You understand me correctly, yes." Gerald retorted.

"You have no issue taking life from them?"

"No."

"Even Elsabe Marais, an Iron Chieftain and a respected woman of nearly thirty-thousands nights in age? What of your sister, Cosette?"

"Elsabe has had her time. My sister is on tour of Tolerbella and won't be present, but I either of them hinder the task, their breath is yours to take."

"What of the Puissant Haute Champion? Would she not be guarding the Elders? Would she not be accompanied by her personal battalion, the formidable Erebus?"

"Zamaya Bellegarde?" Gerald laughed, "Even with your fancy clothes and proper speech, deep down you really are just a shellskin brute, aren't you? No understanding of the politics of our land."

"Please enlighten me."

"Zamaya is formidable in quarrel. She is the Puissant Haute Champion after all. Skilled with Magycs and all of that, sure. But Puissant Haute Champion is a merely a superlative title for 'most acquiescent servant.' She's no more dangerous than any other hunting dog, awaiting a command. As for the Elders, Chieftains, and my sister, they have power now. But power, like the river, can be diverted. Especially when being squandered by brutes."

"You should not refer to such esteemed women as brutes. Consider my warning a courtesy." the shellskin's voice was colder than the mountains of Ayrsulth.

"You're funny." Gerald smirked, licking his lips. "I don't believe I've ever been threatened before. Especially not by someone of your lowly station. I am the brother of the wealthiest woman in Courbonne. What could a mere shellskin like you possibly do to me?"

"Trust me," the shellskin responded calmly, "That is a question you do not want me to answer."

"Now you're boring me." Gerald let out an exaggerated yawn, "You are unarmed. And though large in build, with your first step towards my throne, I'd simply clap my hands and this room would be full of attendants with swords and spears drawn. They'd take your breath before you could get within striking distance."

"Perhaps." the shellskin shrugged, "Though now I believe that I have sufficient confirmation."

"Confirmation of what?" Gerald rolled his eyes.

The shellskin extended his right hand and swung it in a circle. As his arm moved, his muscle fluttered, and the features of his face contorted and trembled. Within moments the transformation was complete. The shellskin was gone. Their true identity was revealed.

"That you, Seigneur Gerald, plot not only against family, but all of Javari." Zamaya Bellegarde snarled, as tongues of Magyc flames danced from her fists, their red-gold light reflecting in the horrified eyes of Gerald.

-7-

Kyrian woke up in covered in sweat. He shivered and tightened his cloak around his shoulders. He had nodded off again. During his waking moments, he tried not to dwell on previous endeavors- not because they were grisly, but he simply couldn't see any point in looking backwards. But when his body surrendered to the inescapable grasp of sleep, all he could do was dream of past tasks.

He drew his shoulders up and blew on his hands. Kyrian had been cold before, hell, during his Youth he lived on the outskirts of Tolerbella, with nothing but crippling hunger to protect against the elements. He'd been aware of Verglas, but the stories didn't do it justice. The chill relentlessly sought out any exposed skin. The bitter breezes sank their numbing fangs down to the bone.

Marie was similarly miserable, but it was too cold to complain. She pulled the cork from the frosty wineskin of fermented milk, took a swig, and buried herself beneath the supply tarp in the back of the cart. Even fully dressed, and covered with the makeshift protection, she still shivered violently. The heavy layers of goatskin were no match for the exceedingly brutal tenacity of the climate. She drained the wineskin, squeezing every drop of booze from the canteen, and hugged herself tighter.

Kyrian snapped the reigns. The crack of leather against their backsides drove Brie and Burgundy to charge harder up the gentle slope of the path's incline. An expedition out with thousands of warriors and supplies should've been easy to track, but the trail had gone cold, literally, and figuratively. Now, they were travelling blind, with no other choice but to move forward.

"I was wondering when you'd wake up." Marie yelled tipsily through her chattering teeth, as she tossed the empty wineskin out of the cart, "That's the last of it."

"Getting drunk won't help anyway." Kyrian replied, "It thins the blood. Protein would be better."

"Well, we're out of meat too." Marie belched, "We'll probably have to eat Brie and Burgundy."

"That's not funny." Kyrian shot his shivering companion a steely look.

"It wasn't supposed to be." Marie yawned, pulling the tarp around her ears.

"Marie…" Kyrian's tone was ominous.

"If we were lower down the mountain, this wouldn't be an issue. We could trap some tri-horn goats or catch a few vermin to roast. Hell, I'd bet those trees back there were full of akokono."

"We're not eating Brie and Burgundy!" Kyrian snapped, "It's almost sun-fall. We'll go as far as we can now, then find shelter for the night."

"It's been too many nights." Marie scowled, "This task is beginning to feel more like a fool's errand."

"Indeed." Kyrian responded flatly, "But say another word about eating Brie and Burgundy, and my club will loosen your teeth and flatten your skull. I'll cut your throat and invite my beasts of burden to join me as we dine on your innards. Zebras aren't food…they're zebras."

"No need to get so emotional." Marie drunkenly apologized, slumping down in the cart.

"Look!" Kyrian pointed, "See that there along the roots of the trees."

A layer of mucus coated the base of the barren trees lining the sides of the path. The milky-grey slime was wider than four carts. It contrasted against the matte textures of the black frost and brown roots.

Kyrian pulled the reins, halting Brie and Burgundy. He climbed down from the cart and cautiously approached the trail, taking great care not to step in, or otherwise disturb the viscous discharge.

"Carcolh." Marie whispered.

"Haven't we dined on carcolh flesh before." Marie fingered her throwing daggers, "It wasn't pleasant, but it would sustain us."

"Yes, we have." Kyrian agreed wincing "But the carcolhs we ate before were just juveniles. They were small and weak, probably escaped from some Magyc creature peddler. But do you notice the width of the slime trail there, near the base off the trees?"

"I see it." Marie nodded hungrily.

"That's twenty times the size of those we ate before. This carcolh would be at least the size of a war elephant. Body like a sea serpent, the crest of its shell would be as tall as you, and the quills flung from the barbed tentacles protruding from its eyeless face would be as long and thick as my arm."

"So what?" Marie licked her lips, "More meat."

"Not to mention that its trail leads down that slope. To track it now would put us at a severe disadvantage. Even if we were able to subdue the creature, merely tracking it would add at many nights to our task."

"Just as well," Marie shrugged, "As repulsive as those small ones were, I'd rather eat chacal droppings."

"Well my discerning friend," Kyrian pointed, "If that's what I think it is, you just may get your wish."

A few hundred yards ahead, the path narrowed slightly as it reached a plateau. On top of that plateau were a dozen, abnormally tall, and disturbingly lanky silhouettes stalking up the hillside towards a bright spot of light.

"Chacals!" Marie gasped.

"An entire pack of chacals." Kyrian whispered, his mild astonishment matching Marie's excited tones.

"But what's that light?" Marie leaned forward, balancing firmly on the edge of the cart. The revelation of shapeshifting beasts had a sobering effect.

"I believe that's the dangerous end of an ignited assegai being wielded quite expertly." Kyrian squinted.

"It must be another shellskin!" Marie held her cloak and jumped off the cart as well, "And if they have an ignited assegai, they must've have taken it from of the expedition members in the group from Tolerbella."

"Precisely." Kyrian snarled deliciously, "Do you have any dried Somnus in your satchel?"

"I do." Marie produced a small paper bundle, undid the tie, and poured flakey orange herbs into her palm.

"Feed it to Brie and Burgundy." Kyrian instructed, "There's no place to hitch, so we'll put them to sleep."

"What do you think?" Marie asked, feeding Brie and Burgundy the sedative plants, "I count twelve chacals, but perhaps the rest of the expedition is lying in wait?"

"If the rest of the expedition were waiting, they wouldn't leave a shellskin alone. If not for their oaths of protection, then because of strategic advantage in neutralizing two threats at once."

"Perhaps whatever is left of the expedition is too injured to fight further." Marie smiled to herself, drawing a few of her daggers and rolling them expertly in her hands.

"Very astute." Kyrian smiled at Marie, his eyes full of genuine admiration, "Brie and Burgundy are sedated. You seem sober enough. Let's go kill some chacals."

-8-

Orianne swung her assegai in a desperate display of intimidation to keep the gargantuan creatures at bay. A chorus of staccato snarls and growls followed every swing. Two dozen violet eyes stared at her, communicating in chattering utterances as they planned their attack strategy through grossly indecipherable vocalizations.

The chacals matched their description in the accounts. Covered in coarse hair that was a blend of dark grey and brown, with long, pointed ears, their eyes remained unaffected by the transformation, but their elongated snouts erased any lasting semblance of humanity.

Though the situation was undeniably dire, Orianne couldn't fully focus on the threat before her. Her mind kept wondering back to Kiyolowe. They had been alerted to intruders on the mountain, but now Kiyolowe and her farfadets were strangely absent.

The chacals maintained their position but kept their distance. Though their ears were flattened against their broad heads, and their backs were arched in a pounce position, they seemed content for now to keep her trapped. It would only be a matter of time before they advanced.

The creature directly in front of her was the leader of the brood. Furry protrusions adorned its bulbous head, which was speckled with black sores amid a patchwork of scars. Faint vapor escaped their jagged nostrils. It was larger than the others and was always the first to let out the distinctively disquieting growl every time Orianne swung her assegai. With every guttural utterance, the other chacals would respond with their own unnerving cries.

The two smaller monsters at the far left and right side of the pack snarled and took a small step forward, fangs barred, thick saliva dangling from their jaws. Th elongated fingers of their gnarled hands outstretched, they retreated quickly when Orianne swung her spear again, narrowly missing their glistening muzzles.

"They're toying with me." Orianne irritably muttered to herself, allowing her anger to overtake her fear.

Orianne tore the cloak from her neck and held it against the ignited tip. The cloth instantly burst into flames. She threw the flaming garment in the face of the beast, the fiery cloak ensnaring the creature in an incendiary mask.

The chacal yelped, briefly transforming back into human form as the smell of burning fur and flesh filled the air. The creature lashed about and tossed away the flaming cloak before the fire could do any real damage. Orianne caught a glimpse of its human state, locking eyes with a young boy, who couldn't have been much more than four-thousand nights old.

"They're just Youths!" Orianne whispered under her breath, both astonished and horrified, "What vile, fool-born cretin would wield Magycs against children?!"

Before she could formulate a guess as to who would stoop so low as to betray the innocence of the young with this abomination, two throwing daggers appeared in the side of the youth's head. Howling in pain, he instinctively transformed back into his beastly form, the light from his eyes fading as he exhaled his final breath.

Two more chacals fell. Leather-wrapped hilts protruded from their skulls. The other creatures snarled and howled, as another dagger whizzed by, clipping the ear of the lead chacal, before landing in the hard soil in front of Orianne's feet with a quiet thud.

Like the chacals surrounding her, Orianne couldn't tell where the attack was coming from, but she was thankful for the momentary assistance. She lunged forward, swiping the end of her assegai across the belly of the distracted beast.

The sound of sizzling flesh and smell of singed fur filled her ears and nostrils. It wasn't a fatal strike, but more harmful than she'd anticipated. She was surprised with how quickly her desperation for freedom compromised her abilities. These creatures had wished to take her life and consume her meat. Her calculated defense had devolved into relentless savagery.

A bloody, severed tongue collided with Orianne's shoulder. She looked up to see another chacal fall beneath the knob of a throwing club that had smashed into its head, forcing it to bite off the blackish-pink appendage.

Orianne swiped at anything that growled, careful not to produce any mortal wounds. But as more daggers flew, and more clubs smashed skulls, the dull, black frost of the mountain path was once again awash in the glistening and visceral colors of unnatural death.

When the last of the chacals were slain, Orianne took a knee to catch her breath. She was exhausted and exhilarated, but otherwise unharmed. Staring at the mutilated corpses around her, she marveled again at their comparatively young ages.

In death, the pack of chacals resumed their human forms. For a group to be corrupted by Magycs, wasn't a matter of happenstance. This atrocity was irrefutable evidence of gross and deliberate exploitation.

Orianne wiped her nose and stood. While relieved to still be drawing breath, she reminder herself that it wasn't Kiyolowe or the farfadets that had come to her rescue slinging throwing daggers and clubs.

Gripping her assegai, as she squinted through the gusts of swirling debris. Kneeling beside the corpse of a chacal, she examined the hilts of the throwing daggers sticking out of its face. There was nothing to indicate a region of origin. The throwing clubs were similarly anonymous. The handles were well-worn from use, but otherwise plain. The shafts leading to gore-coated knobs didn't display any distinguishing markings.

Orianne jumped to her feet, ready to engage. She pointed her assegai at Kyrian and Marie, who nodded to her as they around the corpses, collecting their weapons.

"Would you mind handing that to me?" Kyrian extended his hand, motioning for his club.

"Who are you?" Orianne asked, grunting as she lifted the heavy club. She looked up into Kyrian's dark eyes and marveled at his physical dimensions.

Orianne was tall for her age, but even with her statuesque height, the top of her head only reached the lower curve of his broad chest. His huge shoulders appeared even larger with the heavy cloak draped around them.

"My name is Kyrian." he nodded, "This is Marie."

"We've been looking for you." Marie drew up the corners of her mouth, but the smile didn't quite reach her eyes, "Or to be more specific, we've been looking for the expedition you were traveling with."

Orianne turned towards Marie. Though she was significantly shorter, Marie was powerfully built. Even beneath the hefty layers of tightly woven fabrics designed for both warmth and protection, the taunt curvature of her battle-hardened musculature was undeniable.

"Why are your weapons unmarked?" Orianne asked suspiciously, stepping back cautiously from the strange pair, "And what are you doing so deep into the mountains of Ayrsulth, so close to the Time of Verglas?"

"In our profession, we've found it's best not to mark the tools of our trade with regional stripes." Marie answered with a smirk.

"You serve no Stratum?" Orianne exclaimed.

"You can drop the act." Kyrian sighed.

"What act?" Orianne frowned cautiously.

"Oh my!" Marie exclaimed, leaning forward, staring intently at Orianne's face, "Look at those rings on your face! Kyrian, do you see this? Have you ever seen someone with such high honors this far out?"

"Hmm," Kyrian nodded impressed, "Mark of the Three Moon? That's quite a conspicuous disguise."

"I earned all of my marks!" Orianne snapped.

"You must more than be quite skilled then, yes?" Marie continued her invasive examination, "Your assegai bears the stripes of Navanca, but I thought the intellectuals of the Enlightenment Stratum were comprised only of scholars and historians. Was that what you were before?"

"Before? Before what?" Orianne retorted defensively, "I am an Instructor."

As Orianne pondered the odd line of questioning, the piercing howl of the wind was drowned out by the murmuring roar of hundreds of pairs of leathering wings and thrashing tails. A small black spot appeared against the endless canopy of grey clouds. Kyrian and Marie stared in astonishment as the black spot, expanded and grew. It wasn't so much the size of the swarm, but the speed at which they were flying.

Over thousands of nights, and ten times as many tasks, Kyrian and Marie had seen wonders all across Javari. Frozen with awe, they reflexively swam through the multitude of their varied and lengthy memories to try and find some comparable moment but came up short. Within seconds, every speck of sky in their sight was obscured by the unnervingly inhuman racket accompanied by the tremendous, rapidly descending swarm of sixty farfadets.

Half of the farfadets descended, encircling the wide-eyed trio, while the remaining thirty orbited the air, just a few dozen feet above their heads. They were completely surrounded. Orianne turned off the ignited end of her assegai but kept her grip firm.

Kiyolowe dove gracefully through the center of the undulating swarm. The frigid Verglas winds calmly spiraled around her mesomorphic build and sable-colored skin, as if even the cold itself feared her formidable presence.

The ground tremored as Kiyolowe landed in the center of the trio, her wings outstretched. The other farfadets who had preceded her entrance, squatted briefly, then leapt up and took flight, joining the maelstrom of wings and tails swirling overhead. Orianne dopped to one knee, genuflecting to show respect. Kyrian and Marie were awestricken but followed suit.

"You do not belong here." Kiyolowe narrowed her six eyes and snarled, revealing the jagged fangs filling her wide mouth, "Though unwelcome, you are not the intruders my sentries warned me about. Are these more from your expedition, Orianne?"

"The Doyenne speaks in our tongue?" Kyrian gasped in a hushed tone, keeping his head bowed.

"She is not the Doyenne." Orianne whispered back, "She is known as Kiyolowe."

"How do you know her name?" Marie asked shocked by Orianne's casual, authoritative familiarity, "And how does she know your name?"

"Quiet!" Orianne snapped at Marie. Regaining her composure and returning her attention to Kiyolowe, she replied quietly, "With respect Kiyolowe, the large one is called Kyrian. The other is called Marie. They were not part of the expedition. They rescued me."

"Rescued you from what?" Kiyolowe inquired.

"A pack of chacals." Marie answered, "Kyrian and I were riding up to the mountainside and saw Orianne surrounded by a pack of chacals. Fear not though, we silenced their snarls. Perhaps these were the intruders your uh, sentries observed?"

Kiyolowe wasn't quite familiar with the nuances of human facial expressions. She didn't arch an eyebrow, or purse her lips, but the way she quizzically cocked her head and stared at Marie's inexplicably casual retort left no question as to the state of her bemusement. She opened her mouth, and a series of odd staccato clicks and sucking noises filled the air.

Orianne, Kyrian, and Marie marveled at the enigmatically comforting, native tongue of the farfadets. It evoked memories of tall grasses during the warm nights of the planting season.

"My Sistren confirms." Kiyolowe announced.

"Of course they did." Marie shrugged, "Because that is what happened. Perhaps you assume that because I am Javari, that I speak falsely"

"You are strangely confident." Kiyolowe commented.

"My companion isn't confident." Kyrian stood, his voice low, "She's deadly."

"Is that so?" Kiyolowe focused her gaze on Kyrian.

"We have no quarrel with you, Kiyolowe." Orianne interjected, silently pleading with her eyes.

"You do not." Kiyolowe bared her fangs, "But these two, definitely want to exchange more than words. They--"

Kiyolowe's thunderous voice was drowned out by the cries of the shrieking farfadets circling above. Even the harsh gales whipping across Kyrian, Marie, and Orianne's numb ears couldn't dampen the discordant racket resounding off the stone and mud. Kiyolowe reared back and turned towards the lower curve of the path.

Orianne, Kyrian, and Marie watched the amorphous shadow stretch across the rocks, accompanied by a low rumbling growl. The source of the shadows emerged revealing over one hundred abnormally tall, lanky figures. Their eyes glowed above elongated snouts. Their ears were lowered against broad heads. Orianne's stomach tightened as the bewilderingly large pack of chacals advanced.

"A hundred chacals?" Kyrian was astonished.

"Farfadets in the air, farfadets on the ground, chacals blocking the path- I knew Terre d'Os was brutal, but this is ridiculous." Marie quipped.

"Ridiculous or not, we have one hell of a quarrel ahead of us." Kyrian barked.

"Are you with us?" Marie smirked at Kiyolowe, "From what I've heard, you farfadets are particularly fond of these cursed beasts either."

"Are you proposing an alliance with my Sistren?" Kiyolowe responded flatly.

"Just want to make sure while I'm focusing on chacals, when we kill the bastards, I don't wind up with a farfadet talon in my back." Marie spat back.

Before they could cement their tenuous partnership with a verbal agreement, a slender, black spike whizzed past Orianne's ear, striking Kiyolowe in the shoulder. Orianne turned her head as another pair of black spikes punched holes through the center of Kyrian's chest and stomach. He grasped in vain at the gaping wounds as coils of glistening intestines slopped out of his gut onto the dirt.

Orianne and Marie, found themselves bathed beneath a huge and horrifically inhuman shadow. They exchanged trepidatious glances, realizing the farfadets hadn't been shrieking at the approaching chacals.

The severed heads of Brie and Burgundy floated over them. The curved trajectory was marked by an arc of crimson spewing from the ragged holes at the base of their severed necks. Kyrian looked at the dead eyes of his beloved equine, weeping with his final breaths.

Dead trees lining the mountain path folded and collapsed. Kiyolowe yanked the spike from her shoulder and folded her wings down, instinctively caressing the now vulnerable contours of her wheezing frame.

Tears of rage welled in all six of her eyes as the burning power of her commanding echoed out from the pit of her chest. Between erratic breaths, Kiyolowe coughed out a single word…

"Carcolh."

- TUTELAGE LESSON: THE CARCOLH-

The carcolh is a gargantuan, and highly dangerous creature. In addition to its size, the most distinguishing feature is the dense, trochoidal shell. The shell of a fully mature carcolh is roughly the size of a seasonal storage basket, roughly six to eight feet tall at the highest apex of the dome, and stretching between nine to ten feet long, and a diameter of three to five feet at the widest point.

The color of a carcolh shell varies, but usually tends to be some combination of gold, yellowish with white streaks, or pale orange tinged with green flecks. The base and interior of the shell is glossy and pink, radiantly marked or minutely speckled with grey or white. The aperture, columella, and umbilical areas of the immense shell are almost always a pearl silver. The apex of the carcolh shell is acute, and generally eroded from constant brushing against various trees and rocks in its natural habitats among the dusty and arid flatlands of Umadyn, and the treacherous, rocky cliffs of Ayrsulth.

The body of a carcolh appears serpent-like but is actually more closely aligned with that of a snail. The elongated body is more of a large, muscular foot, that uses rapid, sequential contractions to crawl on a layer of viscous slime secreted from glands located all over its body.

Twelve tentacles protrude from the head of the creature, encircling the eye stalks. The tentacles are comparatively short and used primarily to constrict and pull prey into the beast's mouth, though they also seem to serve mildly defensive purposes, keeping brush and debris away from the vulnerable and fragile base the eye stalks.

In addition to these tentacles, carcolh possess the extremely dangerous ability to "throw" quills to ensnare and immobilize prey from a distance. Carcolh quills are comprised of hardened hair-like strands coated in a neurotoxin. Quills are projected from the posterior segment, and are able to pierce stone, bone, and iron as easily as a baker's blade slices through a soft loaf of moistened hand bread. Upon piercing the flesh of the prey, the neurotoxin coating of the quill enters the bloodstream, causing pain, blindness, paralysis, and stoppage of the heart.

While many juveniles have been captured and studied extensively, opportunities to examine fully mature carcolhs have been rare- due to their dangerous nature. Similarly, not much about their origins has been verified, and what little is known is mostly legend.

The most famous description of their beginnings tells of some foolishly lucky Visitants successfully finding carcolh eggs somewhere in their homeland, with the eggs subsequently being lost or stolen somewhere near Umadyn, giving birth to the carcolhs that creep amongst us in the present time.

Tales of Visitants are not to be trusted, but lacking any contradictory evidence, it is the most accepted explanation for how the carcolh- the only Magyc creature that cannot be communicated with- came to be in Javari.

-9-

Barking, screeching, howls, and cries clashed aurally, much in the same way the landscape itself was awash in visceral, bodily collisions and physical entanglements. Hundreds of gallons of blood clouded the wintry air, spraying in all directions from lacerations, gashes, and puncture wounds deeper than the endless pit of fear churning in Orianne's stomach.

The farfadets had tried to keep their distance at first. Using flight to their advantage, they orbited the mountainside, swooping in with talons out and tails thrashing. But the chacals kept coming. Climbing the unforgiving, cold, rocky cliff face, what the furry beasts lacked in aerial superiority, they more than made up for with their preternatural physical agility.

Soon farfadet and chacal alike, were falling over one another and writing in snarling heaps on the floor, biting and kicking, and thrashing about in a horrendous storm cloud of barbs and claws, teeth, and tails.

The chacals were decapitated and disemboweled by farfadet talons. Farfadet limbs and tails were amputated, their wings shredded between the gnashing fangs of chacals. All the while, the immense carcolh thrashed about wildly, flinging spear-length quills that fatally impaled their targets at random.

A steel edge whizzed through the air, missing the tip of Orianne's nose by inches. Ducking, Orianne watched as Marie's throwing knife plunge deep into the open mouth of pouncing chacal. The last sparks of light of life faded from the creature's eyes as it transformed back into a young, human form, collapsing in the frozen soil at her feet.

Orianne stood gripping her assegai in the middle of the fray, a shocked, yet gracious expression peered out from her gore-sprayed face. She quickly mouthing a breathless thank you to her reluctant savior. Marie replied with a curt nod. Marie ducked, yanking a throwing club from the belt of Kyrian's corpse. She swung the heavy melee weapon over her head to deflect the incoming projectile. The arc of the club clashed with the quill, redirecting the trajectory of the spike into the chest of a farfadet nearby.

Through the sweat and tears clouding her eyes, Orianne watched as another chacal was quadrisected by a quartet of farfadets. Before the winged creatures could celebrate their kill, the carcolh lurched forward, flattening them against the rock wall with its ginormous shell.

As she had successfully done in the previous altercation on the mountain path, Orianne dropped low to the ground and sought shelter from the calamitous torrent of sanguinary violence. Crawling quickly, nimbly avoiding the splattered slime of the carcolh trail, she noticed Marie defiantly holding her ground.

Wielding a throwing club in one hand while throwing her knives with the other, partially shielded by the lifeless remains of Kyrian and the Doyenne, Marie racked up a kill count of farfadets and chacals so astonishing, it would put a seasoned battalion of Searchers, Skinners, and Vaincre warriors to shame. But like the fearless soldiers of the Vaincre stratum, Marie's mortal essence was susceptible to the same hazards.

Another carcolh spike flew past, grazing Marie's arm. The jagged edge of the projectile hadn't cut too deeply, but it didn't have too. The toxic coating of the quill had penetrated the skin of her arm. Marie dropped her knives, and fell onto her back next to Kyrian's corpse, squirming and flailing in distress at the contaminated wound.

Orianne stopped crawling. Every ounce of her being wanted to take cover, but she knew that the harrowing situation could only be resolved through death. Whether that death was her own, or that of the carcolh and chacals would be determined by her next move.

Orianne jumped to her feet. Gripping her assegai, she dashed back to Marie, dodging the gnashing jaws of chacals in the short distance between them. Dropping down, she pulled Marie's bad arm to the side, and knelt across it, using her weight as a makeshift tourniquet. Marie yelped, but realized what Orianne was trying to do, and nodded frantically through wet eyes and gritted teeth.

Orianne ignited the tip of her assegai. Orianne deftly flicked her wrist, severing Marie's arm just below the shoulder, the flameless blue heat of the assegai cauterizing it instantly. Marie's eyes widened, then rolled back as she succumbed to the shock. Orianne checked Marie's vitals. She was out cold, but still drawing breath.

Steadying her nerves, Orianne darted over to Kiyolowe. Reaching out her hand, she gently caressing the mighty leader of the farfadets compassionate empathy.

"Orianne," Kiyolowe spat, swatting Orianne's hand away, "See now what your people have wrought upon us?"

"Kiyolowe," Orianne spoke quickly, "I cannot undo the past transgressions of my people."

"This is true."

"There is no question that our act of genocide has rightfully earned your hatred and ire."

"Your attempt to unburden the guilt of your soul means nothing to me." Kiyolowe sputtered.

"Before you read my thoughts." Orianne replied, "You saw my intent. Do so again now!"

Kiyolowe's six eyes frowned. As she read Orianne's mind, the frown melted away, first into astonishment, then understanding so complete, it bordered on forgiveness.

"If you fail, we will die. If you succeed, you might die." Kiyolowe whispered, "But you're still willing, determined even. Your resolve is akin to that of my Sistren. Are you certain that you are Javari?"

"Carcolh are snail-like, but not true snails. Their shells have pockets of air around their internal organs. Transport me within the main chamber of the carcolh shell, and I can subdue the beast from within."

"Your weapon will not be sufficient to penetrate the tough meat of the carcolh heart." Kiyolowe warned.

"Perhaps not." Orianne pointed, "But that is."

Kiyolowe followed Orianne's finger. The Almighty Hellreaver of Hakim Jarrah stuck out of the dirt like a blood-soaked obelisk. Orianne dashed over, and with great effort, withdrew the heavy scimitar from the path.

"This should be sufficient." Orianne remarked.

"What is the saying of your people?" Kiyolowe nodded, "As you have said it, so let it be so."

"Indeed." Orianne smiled, "You said it with such conviction, are you certain that you are a farfadet?"

Kiyolowe smirked and waved her arm. The air around Orianne began to ripple and twist. Orianne waited until the spiral of distortion wide enough for her to jump through.

In a blink, she found herself entombed. Squished between the stomach sack and the rough inner curvature of the shell. The light from the fore blade of the Almighty Hellreaver shone off the reddish-black heart. The heart pulsated erratically. It was large and strong, but not sufficient to sustain a creature of this size. Every moment the creature drew breath was more laborious than the previous. Inhaling deeply, Orianne accepted that the act of mercy fell squarely upon her shoulders. She drove the cutting edge through the tough outer layer of the creature's heart and pulled down, bisecting the pulsating muscle. A flood of warm, inky blue fluid gushed down her throat.

She felt the carcolh shudder and thrash, knocking her about the space within the inner chamber. Drenched and drowning, she yanked the blade down further, ensuring the wound would be catastrophically fatal.

She released her grip and found herself transported again. She was back on the path, kneeling next to Kiyolowe, vomiting out what seemed like a wine barrel's worth of carcolh blood. Weeping with exhaustion and shame, as the last of chacals met their demise beneath the talons of the of surviving farfadets.

"Well done, Orianne." Kiyolowe's voice was barely above a whisper, "Well done indeed. Wipe the fluid from your eyes and behold. The carcolh is slain by your hand."

"And your Magyc." Orianne gagged, spitting the last bits of carcolh blood from her mouth, "I wish there had been another way. I am not keen on shedding blood."

"Considering your cunning mind, that you have such a strong aversion to physical violence is a blessing to us all." Kiyolowe chuckled, coughing violently.

Kiyolowe examined the mountain path. The hardened, frozen soil had been carved into a lacerated latticework, framed with black and red ribbons of blood. The shredded remains of the deceased speckled the unsettled earth. Flesh and fur, muscle and sinew, teeth and bone had been trampled into indistinguishable pools.

The carcolh lay motionless, its gargantuan shell leaning against the mountainside. There was a contradictory beauty about its corpse that offset the horror of its rampage. It was both an abomination and miraculous wonder of nature.

This was not lost on Orianne. In the moment, standing beside Kiyolowe, taking in the horrors, Orianne realized that though the immediate threats had been neutralized with the utmost finality, something far more insidious still remained, threatening the very nature of existence itself.

"For a carcolh to reach that size naturally is unlikely." Orianne remarked, "For chacals to amass in such large numbers is unprecedented. That two abnormalities would appear together cannot be a coincidence."

"I suspect your words to be truer than you realize." Kiyolowe nodded, "Your kind has arrogantly attempted to bend Magycs to their nefarious will for countless generations. But they've never attempted something of this scope, nor tread so brazenly into our lands. Who could possess such unrelenting hubris?"

"Lanos." Marie called out. Her diminutive frame was caked in dried chacal blood. She leaned against Kyrian's corpse, careful not to brush the severed stump of her amputated arm against his toxic flesh. "His name is Lanos."

"You know him?" Orianne cringed.

"No. I don't him." Marie snarled, "But I do know where to find him."

-TUTELAGE LESSON: VISITANTS ORIGINS-

Visitants are a people for whom existence is a constant state of desperate wandering. They came to Javari ostensibly for the purposes of exploration, searching for opportunity, but the reality of their motivations was made apparent shortly thereafter. Much like the parasitic jasmine grubs bursting from the bellies of their hosts, Visitants had consumed their lands through warfare and exploitation, now they had burst free from the confines of their borders, on an imperative mission fraught with anguish and despair.

The Visitant homeland is called Klnesyn. Though many from the Explorateur Stratum have attempted to find it, none have succeeded. Klnesyn is nearly four times the size of Javari. The bleak environment forced the Visitants to gather near the coastal regions, leaving the majority of the continent largely uninhabited.

Based on Progenitor records, the Visitant to successfully lead a group out of Klnesyn was Arthron Goras Balwarin. Balwarin's exodus was not without tragedy. Lacking knowledge of the migratory patterns of leviathans, he piloted his vessel, the White Doloras, directly into the center of a pod of leviathans, during mating season. The ship was ill-equipped to handle the calamitous maelstrom caused by the frenzied couplings of the great sea beasts and was nearly destroyed. When they arrived at Javari, Balwarin shared his account of the horrific tragedy. The following are excerpts from his personal log:

"Infinite Mother, ruler in the skies, I come to you in my times of trouble. Grant me wisdom so I might illuminate the darkness. Magnificent Mother, my guardian, I have a confession to make for I have sinned. I fell from the path and have caused hundreds of my countrymen to fall into the forever sleep at the bottom of a watery pit.

Those of us who survived the massacre of Ubronesya the night before, gathered near the Onamark Caves, where I'd been patching up the White Doloras in secret for many months. I wasn't certain if the vessel would be ready, but the hull was seamless, the main and foremasts were sturdy and reinforced with white tar, and the circumstances of our swift departure negated any misgivings I had about her seaworthiness, no matter how justified they may have been. I mistook my hubris for confidence in my skills, and my penance was the death of innocents.

136

We set out seeking liberty, yet the still waters gave way to unrelenting torrents. The endless beauty of the clouds and sun above were veiled by waves that thrashed against our vessel. It was not a storm that besieged us, but a group of monstrous creatures, the likes of which none of us had ever before witnessed!

Each beast was as long and large as the White Doloras, with a ring of piercing amber eyes encircling their massive heads. They were serpentine, but even with no visible limbs, each were astonishingly nimble, gliding through the rough waters with the ease and agility of hunting dogs chasing down quarry in an open field. Their long necks were beset on four sides by rounded scales and rows of small crystal growths. The skin of the beasts glowed with a hypnotic luster, as brightly hypnotic as the coals pulled from the potter's kiln. The tail ends of the beasts possessed tendril-like growths, from which a knobby mace of spiky bone protruded, covered in the same rounded scales as their bodies.

These knobby bludgeons smashed into the stern, cracking the bow, and knocking the ship sideways. The first blow would've capsized us, had it not been for the impact of another beast, knocking us back the opposite way. We were battered, each collision resulting in dozens flying overboard to be lost in the churning black swells. For three hours, all we could do was pray that the next strike would be our damnation. In the fourth hour of the fracas, it was over. The beasts retreated into the depths.

The surface of the ocean was littered with floating debris and supplies. The ocean foam was awash in red and pink and black. We retrieved what we could and mourned all we lost. It is only through your divine mercy that we weathered the onslaught. Of the eight hundred and twenty who embarked on this quest with me, four hundred and seventy-nine souls were lost..."

When the Visitants arrived. from across the Fleshwater Ocean, they, sought to empower themselves in the name of their cursed homelands. Their home country possessed few natural resources, but those scant blessings of nature were nowhere near the abundant array of flora and fauna native to our lush, vast ecosystems of Javari.

Visitant culture is built entirely on survival, yielding a religious reliance on a spattering of conflicting and confusing customs. Because of disease, famine, and cursed luck, they rely on cunning and superstition. Their society is closer to that of a den of wild tauren lizards than a civilized collective of human beings.

Visitants are extremely distressed. They live bleak lives and have endured enough calamity to last a thousand generations, but their refusal to evolve, and rejection of education is perhaps their most depressingly dangerous trait.

What they lack in natural and supernatural awareness, the more than made up for with their engineering innovations. The bellies of their massive sea vessels contained many strange armaments and advanced technologies. These instruments were similar in design- their slings were still slung, their spears possessed blades- but were vastly different in material. The ingredients of their warcraft came from jars and cauldrons, blending fire with earth to create new elements.

The Visitants were defeated in the War of Progenitors. Their superior weapons were redoubtable, but no match for the combined might of our glorious ancestors. Battle raged one thousand, four hundred and sixty-seven nights, but in the end, Javari were triumphant. The surviving Visitants were humbled. In awe of our exceptionalism, and grateful to be given quarter, the Visitants surrendered unconditionally, and quietly accepted the generosity of the Elders, who allowed them to establish enclaves, along the border of Terre d'Os.

T. AARON CISCO

-10-

Orianne considered herself to be open to new experiences, no matter how daunting of foreign. Squinting against the wind, clinging to Kiyolowe's back as they flew, she decided that a few activities simply weren't for her.

During the early nights of Tutelage, a Pathfinder from the Explorateur Stratum took her class aboard a cartography balloon. The airship was pleasant, gliding gracefully above the treetops. It was the complete opposite of Kiyolowe's high speed arcs, banks, and dives, hundreds of feet above the winding mountain trails.

Gritting her teeth, Orianne looked over to her left at Marie, who was riding on the back of one of the six surviving farfadets. Though the wings and back of the Sistren farfadet was significantly smaller than Kiyolowe, it kept up the breakneck pace. Still, Marie's face was blank, almost stoic. Orianne was envious of her composure.

The nine of them had already been travelling swiftly, turning what had been a forty-night ascent into a three-night journey. Still, they had further to travel before they reached the base of the mountain and The Filet Noir, where Marie claimed they would find the one responsible.

To avoid starvation, every sunset they would land and make camp. Orianne would use her assegai to ignite a fire, and Kiyolowe would provide the Sistren, and their human companions with coppermilk, straight from the slender ducts near the back of Kiyolowe's throat. To allow Orianne and Marie to maintain some small manner of dignity, Kiyolowe spewed the preternatural elixir into her cupped palm, so that the humans wouldn't have to imbibe directly from her mouth like infant birds.

In Tutelage, Javari Youth were taught that farfadets harvested coppermilk the way the lowland bees made honey. The Sistren flew to unknown sources, collected nectar in their talons, and then take it back to the hive, where it was stored and refined into coppermilk.

Seeing the process firsthand, Orianne gained a new respect for farfadets, and understood Kiyolowe's initial distrust. When expeditions went out to gather coppermilk combs, it wasn't like making silk from moth cocoons, or shearing goats for wool. The Javari had nearly erased n entire species, while stealing their primary resource.

Orianne also had to be mindful of her thoughts, as Kiyolowe often responded to her internal queries verbally, embarrassing Orianne on numerous occasions. Marie was less concerned with offense or humility. She didn't marvel at the newfound revelations. She was singularly focused, driven by a perspicacious desire for vengeance. Her mind was full, but not from curiosity.

"We must be getting close, yes?" Orianne yelled over to Marie, wrapping her arms tighter around Kiyolowe.

"Still a bit further!" Marie yelled back, "At this pace, we should be there by sun-fall."

"Perhaps now would be a good time to rest then? So, we are fresh for our confrontation with Lanos." Kiyolowe chimed in, throwing a knowing look of mild compassion over her shoulder at Orianne.

"Thank you." Orianne graciously whispered.

"We'll land here." Kiyolowe broke into a dive. The other farfadets followed suit.

The Sistren farfadets used their talons to slash through branches of the frozen Bulari trees to provide fuel for warmth. Kiyolowe dispensed coppermilk into Marie's wineskin, who in turn poured half into a makeshift calabash for Orianne. Orianne ignited her assegai and set the wood ablaze. When the flames were sufficient, one of the Sistren kept watch as the others gathered around the fire.

143

"Did you notice all the Magyc creatures roaming across Ayrsulth during our travels?" Orianne asked, sipping her coppermilk, sighing deeply as the warm elixir calmed her nerves and rejuvenated her spirit, "The herds of gbahali, the massively intricate webs of the giant J'ba Fofi Spiders, roaming packs of silver-black Ndalawos, a few nights ago I even saw what looked like a clan of Biloko hunting cat-headed snakes. I had no idea Terre d'Os had such a vibrant ecosystem., I didn't realize there were so many Magyc creatures in abundance."

"I didn't realize you could see anything with your eyes closed. And my word, the way you were squeezing Kiyolowe so tightly..." Marie teased.

"While it is true that I wasn't...comfortable, with our travel, I was still aware of my surroundings." Orianne snapped back jovially.

"I don't understand why we had to fly any way." Marie stretched her back and turned toward Kiyolowe, "Couldn't you use your Magycs and transport us instantly."

"My Magycs have become limited." Kiyolowe remarked, staring into the fire, "And the creatures you saw? They are new additions, driven here by the aggressive and careless expansion of your peoples."

"Surely that only part of the reason." Orianne replied, "Javari respects the borders drawn by the Progenitors."

"There is a stark contrast between what your people claim, and what they do." Kiyolowe retorted, "And many of the new additions aren't native to this land. In fact, the imbalance is too great. Their presence is killing the plants and draining the waters. Soon the land of blood, will be the land of death."

"How'd they get here?" Marie asked slurping the last of the coppermilk from her wineskin.

"The one we seek should be able to provide that answer." Kiyolowe replied grimly.

"Your name is fascinating." Orianne broke the tension, "Why do they call you the One-Woman Plague?"

"Kyrian gave me that name." Marie mumbled.

"I am truly sorry for your loss." Orianne replied softly, "I've not experienced the same depth of tragedy, but losing a lover is always—"

"I am a shellskin!" Marie snapped.

"Be that as it may," Orianne nodded respectfully, "you're allowed to grieve those who have taken final breath. Especially those with which we have been intimate."

"Kyrian and I were not intimate." Marie turned her head, "Shellskins do not waste time with such trivialities."

"Sexual congress is a triviality?" Kiyolowe interjected, her voice tinged with surprise, "I thought for Javari, consummation was considered a necessary and sacred act."

"I don't know if I'd say it's…sacred." Orianne chuckled awkwardly, "But it's definitely necessary."

"Only among the Stratums." Marie exhaled exasperated, "They waste much energy on who you should or shouldn't sleep with, whether or not you've slept with too many, or not enough. I've far more pressing concerns than whether the length of my tunic is sufficiently enticing."

"I didn't mean any offense." Orianne apologized, "I assumed that the two of you were…I'm sorry."

"If I want to sleep with someone, I will." Marie softened her tone, "But shellskins do not succumb to base compulsions. And we do not compromise our well-being for the insignificance of momentary pleasures. Kyrian was my partner. He was my friend. As a shellskin, I would never engage in acts of carnality with a friend or partner, but yes- I grieve his death."

"Understood." Orianne demurred.

"It is of little matter. You didn't know." Marie's voice returned to a friendly timbre, "You want to know how I got my name?"

"Yes. Please." Orianne nodded.

"When we first met many, many, many nights ago, Kyrian was due to be executed for perfidious actions."

"Perfidious?" Orianne shrugged.

"It means deceitful." Kiyolowe commented.

146

"Thank you." Orianne smiled, mildly embarrassed.

"Kyrian had accepted a task, but then later learned that the targets of the task were a youth and her dog. Apparently, the dog bit a Patrician just outside of Courbonne. Both child and pet were to be killed for the offense."

"What is a Patrician?" Kiyolowe asked.

"The second tier of the Unir Stratum." Orianne responded, "They are high ranking members of our society, tasked with attending to the affairs of the Queenmothers."

"Such an elevated station wished death upon a child? You Javari are a strange people." Kiyolowe shook her head.

"Kyrian refused to take breath from either, and rather than do the job themselves, the Patrician complained to members of the Amaranthine- the judgement council of shellskins- and for the crime of perfidiousness, Kyrian was set to be scourged and dismembered. As a member of the council at that time, I disagreed with the decision. I was the only one who disagreed with the decision."

"There is indeed honor within you." Kiyolowe stated.

"This was a matter of practicality." Marie ignored the slight insult, "Kyrian should've gotten the details of the task. But during the trial, they listed the impressive feats from his previously completed tasks. Executing a man of his skills would've been a waste of a uniquely talented shellskin."

"I see." Kiyolowe grunted.

147

"But there's more to the story, yes?" Orianne interrupted, "Disagreeing with a decision certainly isn't enough to warrant that horrendous a label. How did he come to called you the One-Woman Plague?"

"Disagreeing with the majority decision is not taken lightly." Marie began, "So to avoid ending up facing the council judgement myself, after casting my vote of dissent, I opened their throats."

"You've opened many throats in your time." Kiyolowe inquired, "I don't even have to read your thoughts to know that. What made the slicing of these throats so notable?"

"They weren't." Marie smiled, "But it wasn't their throats that earned me the title. I had to ensure that there wouldn't be retribution. I learned that the Amaranthine was working with the Unir Stratum. Shellskins were performing questionable tasks under dubious circumstances, no questions asked. In exchange, the leaders turned a blind eye towards our occupation. I didn't become a shellskin to be the lap dog of Courbonne."

"Why did you become a shellskin?" Orianne asked earnestly, "You are educated and eloquent. You possess undeniable skill with your weapons. You are a master of numerous combat arts. Not to mention, you're quite beautiful in appearance. Your talents would've made you legendary within any rank of all the Stratums."

"Almost at our journey's end, and only now it seems you have found your curiosity." Marie replied in a dark monotone, "Perhaps your allegiance to the Stratums outweighs our recent camaraderie?"

"No, I was just—" Orianne stammered.

"Calm yourself. We might die on this quest, and you're worried about offending a shellskin you just met a few nights ago?" Marie answered candidly, stopping to sit on a frozen stump, "I've nothing to gain from secrecy. And besides, if you or your farfadet friends try to kill me when we reach the base, I may not be able to take life from you all, but you Orianne? If there is any treachery, I'll make sure you take your last breath moments before I give my own."

"I did not mean to offend." Orianne whispered, taking a seat next to Marie. Kiyolowe and her sextet of farfadets knelt in a circle around the two warrior women.

"I'm sure you didn't." Marie smiled, "But the last thing you said? My beauty of appearance? I got tired of telling people that there was more to me than my appearance. Instead, I let my work tell them."

"You dedicated your life to murder, just to prove to others you were more than a pretty face?" Orianne gasped.

"Not to others. To prove it to myself." Marie replied.

Orianne fell silent. She was taken aback by how closely she related to this harsh and horrifically violent woman.

"That certainly explains your skills." Kiyolowe quipped, breaking the tension.

"Look, we're pretty close. Since we cannot use Magycs, perhaps it'd be better to finish this journey on foot, so as not to arouse Lanos' suspicions. Orianne can act as my captive, but Kiyolowe, you and the others…"

"Understood." Kiyolowe confirmed, "My Sistren and I will keep watch from above, out of range of his sight."

"Won't his suspicions be aroused by your presence anyway?" Orianne asked, "Even with me acting as your prisoner, won't he have questions for why a shellskin returned from an unfinished task?"

"Good point." Marie frowned and nodded, "Simply telling him that the expedition was successful, will not be enough. But if I tell him there was too much coppermilk to carry, and have you as my prisoner, that gives him little reason to question my word. Give me your calabash. Kiyolowe, can you fill it with coppermilk?"

Orianne handed over her calabash. Kiyolowe nodded, parted her lips, and filled the gourd to the brim, before plugging the stopper and handing it back.

"My Sistren and I will be just overhead." Kiyolowe nodded to the other farfadets, and they took to the skies.

"I hope this works." Orianne walked over and tucked her assegai under Marie's good arm.

"It will." Marie adjusted her baldric of throwing knives, bound Orianne's hands, and lead her down the path.

Just as Marie had predicted, they reached the Filet Noir just as the final rays of the sun gave way to the rich amber dim of dusk. The sky was dark, but visibility along the path was not yet dependent upon starlight. Still, the torches mounted on either side of the door had already been lit.

"Keep yourself to yourself. Ne fais pas?" Orianne read aloud as they passed the signpost at the edge of the clearing, "What kind of tavern is this?"

"Quiet." Marie titled her head back towards the trees.

Orianne looked over Marie's shoulder, squinting at shapes moving along tree line. The shapes grew closer, becoming more distinct. The light from the stars shone just enough that through the frozen flora, it was clear that they were encircled by dozens of Visitants.

"We are surrounded." Orianne whispered, "What now?"

"We fight." Marie responded.

"Ce n'est pas necessaire. That won't be necessary." a heavily accented baritone called out.

Orianne and Marie turned to see Lanos, leaning against the doorway of the Filet Noir.

-TUTELAGE LESSON: VISITANTS FOLKLORE-

The Visitants are a highly superstitious people. While the Jabari base the knowledge on extensive study and are driven by the fundamentals of the observable world, the Visitants conversely rely on strange and outlandish legends, defying even the most forgiving stretches of logic. Consider The Divine Heriot, a cornerstone of Visitant culture. The tale has many variations, the oldest and most popular of which is the following:

Ten thousand generations ago, a brutal warlord named Lyalla Ayil suffered a mortal injury. On her death bed, she contemplated her life of violence, trying to decide if all the carnage she'd wrought truly benefitted the people under her command. After many nights of torment, she concluded that the oceans of blood she'd shed had not left the people better off, and she vowed to spend her every night and day until her last breath trying to undo the unfathomable damage.

Over the next few days, she disbanded her pillaging bands of warriors and split the spoils of her innumerable conquests amongst the people. She melted a hundred thousand suits of armor and dismantled a kingdom's worth of weapons and assorted instruments of death. She used the metal to build farming machines and building tools, musical instruments and artistic effigies, vessels for transporting water and storage houses for grain. She outlawed theft and murder, granted amnesty to deserters, and freed the slaves and prisoners. She decreed that violence of any sort was to be used only in defense of life, and even then, as a final resort.

All of the people celebrated the reforms. All the people but one- her wife, Aurora. Aurora was the thirteenth wife of Lyalla. The previous twelve had been either been killed in battle or succumbed to disease. She was also the youngest, a runaway slave girl, rescued by Lyalla, from the salacious whims of roadside bandits. Aurora was accustomed to her position of wealth and comfort and was displeased with her dying spouse's recent altruism. Lyalla sensed Aurora's displeasure, and allowed her to keep an ivory mortar, she'd gifted her on the night of their wedding.

Aurora grew bored with their humility. And as Lyalla's condition grew worse, Aurora's greed grew, and she took to travelling late in the night to engage in illicit trysts with neighboring warlords, who could provide her with expansive banquets, fine drink, and exquisite gifts.

Sensing her final breaths were drawing near, Lyalla made her hedonistic wife promise that if she remarried, she would not do so with any of the enemy warlords, especially Talaal Budasca, an extremely wealthy, and mercilessly sadistic tyrant. Lyalla went so far as to add, that if Aurora did marry that man in particular, she would return from the realm of the dead, kill Budasca and his men, and grind Aurora's bones into dust, with the ivory mortar, stating that the extreme violence was necessary as it was in defense of the not just one life, but the lives of all the people under their charge.

Fearful, of the curse, Aurora reluctantly agreeing to her Lyalla's request. But five hundred nights after Lyalla gave her last breath, Aurora grew restless, and made her way to Budasca's village. In exchange for a life of luxury, she offered to marry the tyrant, produce numerous heirs, even reveal the location of hidden pathways and tunnels that would allow Budasca to conquer her own people.

Budasca was an old and hideous man, his appearance twisted by his own cruelty. He was not accustomed to being propositioned by desperate women, and immediately accepted the Aurora's terms. He called for his captains in from the fields and tasked his lieutenants to fetch him the most skilled cooks to prepare a lavish wedding feast.

Shortly after the ceremony, as they were sitting down to eat, the ghost of Lyalla appeared before the wedding guests, clutching the ivory mortar in her decaying hands. The howls of the dying echoed throughout the land all night, as ghost of Lyalla tore out the throats of all who were in attendance. Aurora hid herself beneath the table, holding her ears as the spirit fulfilled the curse.

By morning, only two survivors remained, Aurora and a young slave boy, who'd been sleeping nearby in the stables. The young boy was shocked by the bloody scene before him, and even more so, when he witnessed the ghost of Lyalla lift Aurora into the air, tear off her limbs one by one, and grind them beneath the ivory mortar.

Clearly this is nothing more than a fable to teach the value of benevolence and generosity, with a strict warning to uphold their vows. To the Visitants, this tale is not merely a fable, but rather as genuine as any and all of the recorded history of their elders.

-11-

The Visitants stood shivering in the crisp air of the clearing. They didn't react when the one-armed woman pushed through their ranks, brandishing three blades in her good hand. No cries of astonishment or shock were uttered when she buried those knives in Lanos' belly, and then kicked him in the teeth when he hunched over from the excruciating sensation of as the frozen blade points penetrating his navel. As Marie tore through his abdomen and organs, they just watched.

"Before I take your breath," Marie hissed, "You will use whatever Magycs you have left to restore the balance to these cursed lands before the entire continent is destroyed. Refusal will only prolong the inevitable. I will burn your bar and sever the tendons in your arms and legs. I will feed your body to the flames. Your eyes will blister. Your lungs will swell with smoke and burst. You will know true pain."

"Petite femme brutale!" Lanos spat blood, "You are a nightmarish killer, but surprisingly eloquent when it comes to expressing the grisly details of your violence."

"Undo what you have done." Marie's eyes displayed zero evidence of sympathy.

"Je suis désolé." Lanos sputtered, "I am sorry, I cannot undo anything, without first knowing what it is that you think I may have done."

"Forty nights ago, you gave my partner and I a task that sent us into a region you had been manipulating with Magycs. Your manipulations got him killed. I know you can wield Magycs. It would be in your interests to do so now."

"You clearly have mistaken me for another," Lanos grimaced through the pain, "Even if I were the one responsible, how could I restore breath to your companion, when I can barely restore the flesh of my own arm? C'est nes pas logique. It's not logical, no?"

"LIAR!!!" Marie roared. Withdrawing a blade from her baldric, Marie held it high so every soul in the clearing could see. Light glinted off the full length of the weapon. The grip was wrapped in red scaled leather. The blade itself was nearly as long as her forearm, with a wide, asymmetrical base, and wavy, undulating edges that curved from point to hilt like a winding stream.

Lanos raised his scarred arm and bowed his head. Whether or not the Mournblade was actually forged from the fang of the Ninki Nanka didn't really matter. To find yourself on the receiving end was no less horrific.

"I assure you," Lanos whispered through ragged breaths, "I am not capable of what you have said. Though it appears you have made your decision. Ça n'a pas d'importance. It doesn't matter. All I ask is that you spare these Klnovos. They pose no threat and have nothing of value."

"Klnovos?" Marie lowered the Mournblade, and looked around at the witnesses watching in the clearing, "Why do you refer to them as Klnovos?"

"That is what they are." Lanos replied, "It was the Progenitors who labeled them Visitant, to justify the oppression and genocide. Klnovos is their true name."

Kiyolowe and the farfadets descended from above landing gracefully in the clearing. The Klnovos moved back slightly, gripping their children, and holding one another, but otherwise remained silent. The Sistren untied Orianne and took a non-threatening, yet defensive position.

"He speaks truth." Kiyolowe proclaimed placing her hand on the Mournblade, and gently lowering it.

"Perhaps," Marie snarled, "But that doesn't change anything! He is the reason Kyrian no longer draws breath!"

159

"I've never killed anyone, directly or indirectly." Lanos groaned, holding his bloody stomach, "And I am certain that I have never seen any of you before. Though I must say, it is an honor to be in your presence Kiyolowe."

"How does he know your name?" Marie hissed.

"I am Lanos Ndintu-Bel Acqwon. For thirty-two thousand nights, I have sheltered Klnovos at the base of the Ayrsulth mountains, continuing the work of my family. All who bear the name Ndintu-Bel Acqwon have nourished the Klnovos with the generous bounty of the land, but without the compassion of the Sistren, all would have perished."

"I apologize for the confusion." Kiyolowe nodded respectfully, spewing coppermilk into her hands, she smeared the healing elixir across Lanos' wounds, and allowed him to drink from her palm, "We did not see that you were kin to the Ndintu-Bel Acqwon family until you crawled into the light. We would have intervened sooner if we had known."

"Your humility honors me." Lanos replied, his voice regaining strength and confidence as his wounds healed, "While the accusations are false, they are still quite serious."

"I don't understand." Marie growled, "You know him?"

"The Ndintu-Bel Acqwon family is an honorable one." Kiyolowe began, "We have worked with them since the first humans arrived in Terre d'Os."

"Lies!" Marie cried, "I was here, with Kyrian, Forty nights ago! Lanos tasked up with tracking an expedition! He tested our skillset by having us take breath from dozens!"

"It cannot be." Lanos shook his head.

"Yes!" Marie roared, "We took breath from all the champions of uh…what was her name? Cedonia Barkridge! I took her eyes, and then watched you crush her skull with your bare hands!"

"You took my eyes? a raspy voice called out.

Marie and Orianne turned to see a decrepit old woman in a raggedy cloak saunter out from the clearing. Each step was labored, as though any moment she would collapse. Marie's eyes grew wide in astonishment as she gazed upon the face of Cedonia.

"That's impossible!" Marie cried, "She had a cadre of champions, celebrating the killing of a child they said was a picot. We dispatched them all, with Lanos delivering the killing strike to Cedonia, crushing her head in his arms. He then went on to explain that demonstration is far more convincing than explanation."

"La vérité émerge." Lanos explained, "The truth is clear. You were tricked by Miragem, a false vision. To wield Magycs at that scale are beyond my abilities. But what you said, demonstration is more convincing than explanation?"

"That's the creed of Courbonne." Orianne gasped.

"Oui." Lanos nodded, "Many from Courbonne wield Magycs, but there are few so powerful to wield such a convincing deception. That would require the wielder to be both extremely gifted and harbor an unfathomable amount of hatred and disregard for living souls."

"From my distasteful experiences with those people, it could be any one of them." Marie snarled, "It's time the Unir Stratum learned firsthand why I am the one-woman plague. I will take breath from everything that breathes, and scrape the fat flesh down to the bone beneath the unforgiving curves of the Mournblade. I will dine on their flesh and flood their gilded streets with the blood of their children. All will cry out in torment. All of them."

"Not all, Marie." Orianne interrupted Marie's graphic monologue, "Just one."

"Who?" Marie barked.

-TUTELAGE LESSON: ZAMAYA BELLEGARDE-

The final prophecy of the Progenitors states that when the moon rises from the western skies, and cast a warm, red light upon the southern coasts, a marked child shall stand where the wind meets the tide, and through vicious acts of brutal altruism, bring forth both the end and the rise of nature.

After hundreds of generations, and innumerable false declarations, all of The Iron Chieftains, the Gold Chieftains, the Elders, the Queenmothers of Tolerbella, Ardwood, Navanca, and Courbonne, as well as all of The Mentors and Dominies agree, and the Bronze Chieftain herself have declared that Zamaya Bellegarde is the marked child spoken of in the prophecy.

Zamaya Bellegarde is known throughout the four stratums as the Puissant Haute Champion of Javari. Born into squalor, she rose to the highest echelons of acclaim through the sheer force of will. Much of Zamaya's early life as a Youth has been lost to the passage of time, but what is known is no less astonishing.

During Tutelage, all three of her parents contracted the pox. She took a sabbatical to care for them. Though her recovery efforts were commendable, her parents ultimately succumbed, saddling the orphaned Zamaya with massive debts. Lacking the resources to so much as fill clothe her back, or fill her belly, the young Zamaya had no other option than to abandon Tutelage,

With no possessions, no money, and no vocational path to follow, she scrounged for whatever she could find, even scratching out a living as a shellskin. Lacking a Stratum, it was hard to find a steady stream of clients as she got older. Eight thousand, seven hundred and sixty nights after her birth, she found herself on standing on the cliffs of Lavoi, contemplating taking her own life, when she had a vision of a warm, red light shining over the western horizon. She followed that light to the far coast, swimming to the rocky shores of Calheim Isle, the man-made atoll that at the time, was used to train warriors to fight in the Croyantes.

Though outlawed now, the Croyantes was a barbaric sport dating back to the time of the Progenitors. Groups of fighters competed to see who the best among them was, which in turn meant that they were declared chosen by the ancestral gods. Victory was obtained only when you had plucked out the eyes of your opponent. While the average success of a Croyantes combatant is exhausted after a dozen or so skirmishes, Zamaya competed in over seventy. And as you may recall from any of the numerous, recent portraits, she still has both of her eyes.

Her successes with the Croyantes was due to her near-feral upbringing. It gave her a reputation that spread throughout Javari. Over time, that reputation reached the ears of the Elders and Chieftains, who allowed her an opportunity to become a Schemer, the second tier of the Vaincre Stratum, without going through the rigors of Tutelage.
Zamaya shocked the Chieftains and Elders by asking for one hundred nights to consider their offer.

One the morning of the one hundredth and first day, Zamaya returned to the Elders, covered in a litany of old and fresh wounds, and politely declined, instead requesting to be placed as an Attendant, the lowest rung of the Unir Stratum. The Elders were puzzled, but the Bronze Chieftain saw something within Zamaya, and granted her request, and over many hundred nights, served as a mother figure to Zamaya.

The hundred nights spent in contemplation are the subject of ongoing debate amongst all the tiers of the Enlightenment Stratum. Zamaya herself has declined to provide a detailed account of the period. She has on occasion, upon request from a Chieftain, offered a few glimpses into her incredible sabbatical.

At the start of her first night of contemplation, she heard a voice saying to go and seek out a tauren lizard missing an eye. It took her many nights, but she came across such a tauren lizard, near the edge of the western-most islands of Javari, where Tolerbella's northern border meets the southern wilds of Umadyn. She stalked the half-blind creature for another twelve nights, waiting for a sign, when suddenly the tauren lizard burrowed into the black sands, laid three purple eggs into the pit, and died on the beach. Zamaya skinned the mother, and consumed the eggs, when she had a vision that lasted thirty nights.

In the vision, she saw a race of men who were unlike men. They walked and talked as Javari but were able to commune with the ancestral gods as a Youth speaking to a mentor. These men could cast a rock into the sea, and say, "bring forth food," and moments later, the beach would be covered in all manner of fish and squid. The men could slap a tree in the morning and say, "bring forth shelter," and by night fall, an entire village would spring forth. These men who were unlike men embraced Zamaya and taught her to wield Magycs.

When her training was complete, the men who were unlike men told her to return to Javari and serve her people. After bidding farewell, the men who were unlike men walked into the sea, never to be seen again, and Zamaya walked back to Courbonne to address the Elders.

Though she was the lowest tier of the Unir Stratum, she was more skilled than everyone in the Stratum. She quickly rose through the ranks and was given special permissions to travel between the regions. Whether leading the Vaincre into battle, accompanying the Explorateur on reconnaissance, providing consultation to the Enlightenment, or weighing in on political matters in Courbonne with the Unir, her generous spirit, unmatched skills, and boundless wisdom has allowed Javari to overcome any and all obstacles, thrive under the most challenging hardships, and prosper beyond the wildest dreams of the Progenitors.

-12-

Zamaya didn't sleep well. She was constantly interrupted by coughing fits and chills. She felt better now, though occasionally, she had to brace herself for a painful sneeze. She threw on a robe and ducked out into the cold night, quickly crossing the distance between the embroidered flaps in back of her marquee tent, and the clay walls and thatched roof of the egg-shaped latrine.

Stepping onto the corrugated footrests on either side of the porcelain squat pan, she hiked up her robe and tunic, crouched down, and emptied her bladder. When she finished, she grabbed a handful of bamboo sheets to clean herself, and discarded the used strips in the clay disposal bin. Standing and readjusting her nightclothes, she ladled a few scoops of coconut coir into the squat pan, being careful to cover the sloped bottom, and returned to her tent.

Standing in the entryway, she paused for a single contemplative moment. Turning her head, she scoffed at the decadence. Sumptuous garnet rugs protected her feet from the hard ground. A lattice work of ropes stretched overhead between the support poles of the heavy canvas roof and walls. Heavy skins and tapestries hung from the ropes, adding additional layer of privacy, as well as insulation against the frigid winds.

Her oversized trail cot was large enough to sleep three men. Sturdy cords of palm twine, three-fingers thick, stretched between the hollow but sturdy frame, supporting a thick mattress stuffed with unrefined yak wool. The sides of the cot were curved slightly inward, a result of both intentional design, and countless nights of heavy use. The cot was covered in plush warm blankets and soft linens and rested beneath an ornate baldachin. The ceremonial canopy was embroidered with prayers of protection and triumph.

Zamaya had been isolated within the Marquee Tent. Her muscles ached and her shoulder dropped from the weight of the stress. The region's storage coffers were almost empty, and Courbonne had already sent and lost fourteen prior expeditions. She hadn't been officially tasked with leading a battalion out, but the need was too great to sit around waiting for the bloated gears of politics to grant approval. She did what needed doing.

The two-hundred souls that accompanied her on this mission traveling deep into Terre d'Os, did so willingly, and would follow her every command without question or hesitation. The food supply was exhausted two nights ago, and the water and fermented milk would quickly follow suit.

With the Verglas preventing them from progressing into Ayrsulth, they'd been forced to hold their position at the base of the mountains. Zamaya knew that while boredom could be tolerated, hunger was a particularly lethal foe. She was confident however, that the battalion would give their last breaths for her. That was reason enough alone, to harden her resolve. They would die for her, and in exchange, it was her duty to keep them from doing so.

She sat on her cot and slipped off her boots. The soles had worn thin, and her feet were covered in blisters. She waved her hand and healed her sore toes. She knew it was imprudent to waste Magycs on such a trivial discomfort but couldn't risk the maladies becoming more serious.

She could've easily sent couriers to fetch her palanquin, and then had some of the Searchers carry her on for the duration of the mission. But as a former soldier herself, she knew that a leader who cannot walk would not be respected. She gazed through the entry flaps of the tent, at a growing spot on the horizon. Her valet, Albert Eunice walked up the path and entered the tent.

Many of the Vaincre let their hair grow long, but Albert had kept his black and grey curls neatly coiffured to reveal his thin, menacing face. His beady, bloodshot eyes, set deeply within their sockets, seemed to never blink, and unlike other men of his age, he refused to grow a mustache or beard, opting instead for a tidy patch of white whiskers on the tip of his chin.

His sharp facial features and meticulous hair style offered a stark contrast to his boxy frame. His bloodline was lofty, with family ties running back to the Progenitors, as evidenced by his handsome face, but his figure was closer to that of a brutish outlaw from Tolerbella, making for a disorienting contradiction.

"Enter, Albert." Zamaya waved him in, "Tell me you have good news."

"Mother Zamaya," Albert bowed his head, "The courier scouts have returned, but I regret to inform you that another expedition has been confirmed lost."

"Are you certain?"

"Yes, Mother Zamaya." Albert nodded, presenting the Almighty Hellreaver. The storied weapon was covered in dried blood, and speckled with crusty remnants.

"That was indeed the expectation, but still quite unfortunate." Zamaya sadly bowed her head, and inspected the weapon, "Is that the Hellreaver?"

"Indeed, it is."

"The blade wielded by Hakim Jarrah?"

"One in the same."

"If Hakim Jarrah's expedition has been lost, perhaps our efforts are in vain." Zamaya resigned, lowering her eyes.

"Indeed, Mother Zamaya." Albert bowed, "But there is more to divulge."

"Do tell."

"The courier scouts claimed to have seen the Almighty Hellreaver from the within the carcass of an abnormally large carcolh." Albert arched a knowing eyebrow.

"Were their suspicions aroused?"

"No, Mother Zamaya. They are but Youths, lacking the experience or knowledge to question such discoveries."

"Still. It would be unwise to leave anything to chance." Zamaya sighed morosely, "Bind their hands and gag their mouths. Lead them back into the mountains. Go swiftly, they will be transformed by first rays of the morning light."

"As you have said it, so let it be so." Albert quickly darted out of the tent.

Zamaya reclined back on her cot. A low buzzing caught her attention. Glancing up, she saw a dung beetle circling down from the tent ceiling. Its stubby round body glinted metallic dark blue. It landed at the edge of her cot, folding its wings under its protective shell.

Zamaya leaned forward and examined her miniscule guest. The exoskeletal shell was free from any imperfection. Then she noticed the bug's legs. Zamaya dashed off of the bed and took a knee.

The beetle twitched and shuddered. The tent was filled with the horrific sounds of cracking bones and the unmistakable rustle that accompanied the friction of flesh against flesh, meat against hair. In an instant, the transformation was complete. The beetle was gone, replaced by a regal figure of authority. Zamaya raised her gaze to Cossette Archambault, the Bronze Chieftain.

Her white hair was coiffed in a beautifully intricate web of complex braids, leaving a mesmerizing contrast against the rich umber complexion of her chiseled, radiant face fully revealed. Her majestic cloak was trimmed with bronze ribbon and covered in intricate embroidery.

Her robe was partially open, allowing full sight of the white silk lining and burgundy gomesi, a traditional dress tied with a wide, silk belt worn high around her waist. Below the belt the solid print of the bodice flowed into a wide, patterned of dazzling colors and designs. The sleeves of her were wide and long hiding the heavily jeweled bracelets covering her forearms from elbow to wrist.

"My Chieftain." Zamaya averted her gaze respectfully, "To what do I owe this honor?"

"I have known you for thousands of nights, Zamaya." Bronze Chieftain began, her voice cold yet cordial, "Yet I am still in awe of your observational prowess. No matter the guise, you have always been able to identify me. What betrayed my Metamorphosis this time?"

"It was the legs, my Chieftain." Zamaya responded, "Dung beetles have heel spurs on their hind legs. You did not. It was a small but telling detail."

"Ah, and this is why some refer to you as the first among the living." Bronze Chieftain smiled, "Please. Rise. There is much we have to discuss."

The Bronze Chieftain extended her arms, quietly imploring Zamaya to stand. She did so, and the two most powerful women in all of Javari embraced warmly.

"How may I be of service, my Chieftain?" Zamaya asked, as she and the Bronze Chieftain sat down on the edge of the cot, "I apologize for taking the battalion out, but had I waited for an end to the debates on the council, then—"

"Apology trumps permission." the Bronze Chieftain waved her hand dismissively, "And it is I who owe an apology to you, for not thanking you sooner for handling the unsavory business with my brother."

"My condolences for the loss of kin." Zamaya placed her hand over her heart, "But I am honored that you entrusted me with such a sensitive matter."

"Your work speaks for itself. And thus, we have come to the purpose of my visit, another sensitive matter."

"Yes, my Chieftain."

"Javari needs to evolve. At the end of every Tutelage season, barely any Youths pledge to Unir, and those that do possess mediocre talents. They are hardly fit to rise to even the mid-tier of the Stratum. The strongest pledge to the Vaincre. The smartest pledge to Enlightenment. The bravest pledge to Explorateur."

"Was is not the Progenitors themselves who established the Stratums?" Zamaya asked.

"Truth." the Bronze Chieftain replied, "But our ancestors intended the Stratums to be reflective of a calling, not a mark of identity. The warriors of Erebus camped outside your tent are pledged Unir but would've found success with the Vaincre. The Mentors of Ardwood are Explorateur, but their insights and creativity would be an asset to the Enlightenment in Navanca. The Iron and Gold Chieftains throughout the lower regions possess leadership traits we seek in Courbonne. The other regions have become ill-equipped to handle the mundane challenges of their day-to-day existence, and the arrogance of our own Stratum threatens our authority. So many seek nothing more than personal acclaim, not realizing that a thriving people are more easily ruled."

"Indeed, my Chieftain." Zamaya nodded, "But it is not our nature to prioritize self?"

"Is it?" the Bronze Chieftain exhaled, "You are but a few generations ahead of the most current season, yet even with your divine gifts, and fulfiller of our sacred prophesy, you still recognize that value of the collective. I heard the accounts of what transpired at the last Ritual of Avenir. I can't recall a more impassioned report. The Chief Mentor wrote it. I forget his name. The albino Venturer."

"Alexandre."

"Yes, that's it! Alexandre." the Bronze Chieftain smiled ever so slightly, "When we heard of one with such talents petitioning for a less ideal Stratum, you were dispatched immediately to sway her. However, you allowed her to retain her desired Stratum, but insured she would be sent where her skills would be most useful."

"I beg forgiveness if I acted out of turn, my Chieftain."

"On the contrary, Zamaya. Perhaps if more in Courbonne shared your passion, and willingness to do whatever it takes, we would be able to change our fortunes much more rapidly."

"Your words flatter me, my Chieftain. With all respect, I don't think you came here to compliment my tenacity."

"Indeed."

"How may I be of service?"

"We're dealing with some rather pressing issues." the Bronze Chieftain's carried a grave tone.

"Pressing in what way?"

"Livestock in Navanca have been ensnared in J'ba Fofi webs. Crops in Ardwood have been infested with bloodfly larvae. And due to the malevolence of my departed brother, Courbonne still has yet to see a single child born."

"As per your wishes."

"Indeed." the Bronze Chieftain removed her robe, and leaned forward matching Zamaya's gaze, "But the Iron Chieftains, the Gold Chieftains, Elders and Queenmothers from all the cities and villages in all the regions are beginning to question whether Courbonne can still provide the necessary protections to ensure the Javari way of life."

"They speak of treason?" Zamaya remarked coolly.

"Not yet." the Bronze Chieftain arched an eyebrow, "They are just whispers now. But given time, the softest whispers reach many ears. We need the Veil of Bone."

"My plans were to seek out Skinner Hakim's expedition. Surely my successful acquisition of coppermilk will calm their fears, without the Veil?" Zamaya asked hopefully.

"It may be wiser to journey to Umadyn and eliminate the Visitant threat entirely. Javari will praise our victory, and those who harbor doubts or ask questions, would hold their tongues, fearing similar reprisal."

"You suggest genocide?" Zamaya tried unsuccessfully to mask the surprise in her voice.

"I suggest taking whatever measures are necessary for the prosperity of our people." the Bronze Chieftain nodded pensively, "Did you hear about Tolerbella?"

"What happened in Tolerbella?"

"Reports of chacals ravaging villages loyal to my station. All the ironworkers and swordsmiths of Avolire and Nysisse are dead. The weavers and potters of Lonmut and Chagnon are dead. Four villages, fourteen thousand souls, all lost."

"Perhaps the chacals have strayed from their usual hunting grounds, and tragically found new quarry?"

"Or perhaps the Puissant Haute Champion of Javari has wavered in her devotion?"

"My Chieftain, are you implying that I had something to do with the killings?"

"Do not feign ignorance!" the Bronze Chieftain cast off her robe and clenched her fist. Her hands glowed with the cold light of Magyc fire.

"My Chieftain?"

"The are not many among us who wield Magycs at all, let alone possess that level of skill! Fewer still even know the proper way to wield the Magyc and turn man to beast. There is only one would be so arrogant as to believe they'd get away with such a grave transgression!"

The Bronze Chieftain stared at Zamaya, searching for a sliver of humility at having been discovered.

"Clever old sprite." Zamaya laughed defiantly.

"How dare you address me so!"

"Your abilities are dwindling. Look now, at how your hands tremble just wielding the fire of Martyrr. See how you struggle to maintain those pathetic, meager flames!"

"You shall pay for your insolence!"

The Bronze Chieftain lashed out, punching Zamaya in the chin with her fiery right hand. The impact was fierce enough to shatter stone. Zamaya yawned as the blow bounced off her chin.

The Bronze Chieftain's eyes grew wide, as someone grabbed her from behind. The arms of her captor squeezed against her brittle ribs. Her ancient muscles ached as she struggled against the grasp of the unknown assailant. She felt the fine hairs of her back and shoulders being uprooted. To her horror, she realized, she could no longer feel the weight of the invisible talisman she'd been carrying.

Wrenching herself free, she whipped around to see another Zamaya standing in the center of the tent, her arms sagging beneath the weight of the imperceptible artifact. The false Zamaya sitting on the edge of the vanished. The Bronze Chieftain quickly waved her hands, casting a wield of protection.

"The Veil of Bone." red and gold flames churned in Zamaya's eyes, as drew her arms up and around her shoulders, wrapping herself in the invisible Veil. "So that is how you discovered my intentions? Take solace in knowing your observations were correct. Javari does need to evolve. You mentioned that the Stratums were to be reflective of a calling. That is true. Collective identity is a deceptive shroud, blinding us from what truly matters."

"And what does your twisted mind believe truly matters?" the Bronze Chieftain lashed out again. Dashing around the marquee tent, the Bronze Chieftain hurled skull-sized orbs of Magyc flame. Each fireball found its target but dissipating impotently upon contact with the veil.

"Javari. Visitant. Terre de Sang. Terre d'Os. Empty titles for empty minds. The Stratums are obsolete. The regions are obsolete. We are one land and shall be ruled as such."

"And you believe that you are the one to rule?" the Bronze Chieftain retorted angrily, realizing she had been drawn into a quarrel with no chance of victory.

"Enough!" Zamaya huffed.

Under the wield of protection, the Bronze Chieftain's skin was tough, but Zamaya kept pressing. Powered by the Veil, Zamaya's fingertips pushed through the Chieftain's upper chest. The Bronze Chieftain cried out in anguish. Her will wavered and finally broke.

The Bronze Chieftain's skin cracked beneath the tips of Zamaya's curled fingers. Zamaya continued to push, until the palms of her hand was bathed in viscous warmth. She felt her nails scratch against the rigid contour of vertebrae. The sound of splintering bone echoed through the encampment as Zamaya withdrew her hand, tearing through the muscle, skin, and organs, wrenching the old woman's ribs and spine out into the early morning air.

-TUTELAGE LESSON: MAGYCS-

The Magycs are a powerful force allowing the user, known as a wielder, to harness preternatural abilities to create and control extraordinary wonders. Due to the volatile and potentially devastating nature, only a select few from the Unir stratum are allowed to learn the necessary skills to wield. Although heavily restricted, it is necessary for all who complete Tutelage to have a rudimentary knowledge of Magycs.

The Progenitors learned to wield Magycs from the creatures of Terre d'Os. Those strange beasts are the only known entities who possess the natural ability to wield. The Progenitors graciously accepted the gifts, and in their wisdom, devised the system of training enabling the gifts to be passed down through generations to our current time.

The Magycs as we know them, were originally deemed the First Five. They comprise the building blocks of the gifts. The more experienced the wielder, the more powerful the wield. Most trained in the Magycs are skilled at wielding one or two of the First Five. The more experienced wielders become proficient in three and can combine wields with miraculous results.

Martyrr- a wield enabling the wielder to conjure devastating fire

Manifest- a wield the produces inanimate objects, the stronger the wielder, the larger and more complex the objects being manifest can be

Miragem- a wield the creates hallucinations and visions that are indistinguishable from reality

Metamorphosis- the ability to change the physical characteristics of a living creature. The most advanced wielders can use it to change their own physical characteristics.

Maladie- the most challenging and arduous of wields, Maladie allows the wielder to heal themselves or others of any physical and/or medical affliction. This wield is as powerful as it is beneficial, and because of its incredible nature, has been known to cause irrevocable physical and mental stress and damage upon the wielder.

One famous example of combining wields comes from Ervin Bibek, the skilled Patrician who preceded the predecessor of the current Iron Chieftain of Ardwood. When Ervin was shipwrecked off the southern coast, stranded on a barren island, he combined the wields of Manifest and Martyrr to create a campfire that provided warmth for twenty nights without needing fresh wood.

Another example can be found in the Battle of Cécité. During the Siege of Burning Wind, when the Visitant Rogues briefly gained the upper hand against the Progenitor forces, Skinner Joko Moir snuck across the enemy lines, causing the Visitants to chase her towards the hornet Olobola wetlands. It was mating season for the speckled hornets, and Joko Moir wielded Metamorphosis and Manifest to turn the frenzied swarms of hornets into a bloodthirsty army of giant men, used Miragem to render them invisible. When the Visitant Rogues caught up with her in the swamps, used Manifest once again to change the air itself into a wall of fire that she then used Martyrr to drive the Visitant Rogues back into the spear points and bladed edges of the invisible army.

It has been said that once every few thousand generations, it may be possible for a wielder to master all of the First Five, utilize the 120 possible combinations to create a sixth wield, rendering the wielder godlike abilities to bend the laws of existence and reality itself.

-13-

The path was silent save for the chattering of teeth and the crunching of the frost beneath their soles. Over a hundred Klnovos volunteers joined Lanos, quietly trudging behind Orianne and Marie for the past ten nights. Most of the Klnovos were strong, young, and agile, but there were quite a few elders that could barely hold the weapons Lanos had conjured to arm them. Their minds weighed heavy with the burden of their task. No words were needed.

Orianne had been unnerved by their stoicism, but still relished the serenity of the march. She'd suggested they cross at Passerelle, the artisan village just beyond the walls of the Outpost Cèdon, on the promontory overlooking the inlet between the eastern shores of Ayrsulth and western walls of Courbonne. It wasn't the most tactically advantageous spot, but it was the least heavily guarded, and as such, the most likely to yield a successful entry.

Kiyolowe and her Sistren soared just a few arms' lengths above. They glided so low, that the tips of Kiyolowe's leathery wings occasionally brushed the top of the Marie's head. It had been Marie's suggestion that they fly higher to keep watch, but Orianne rejected the idea, stating that darkening the sky with seven farfadets significantly increased the risk of being spotted by both the watchguards manning the outer ramparts and parapets encircling Courbonne.

"These Visitants don't speak much." Marie griped, swatting at Kiyolowe's wings with her good arm.

"Klnovos." Orianne replied.

"Right. Klnovos. They don't speak much."

"What would you have them say?"

"I don't know. Clearly most of what we'd been told about them was false. But there had to be some truth to the records, yes? Aren't you curious as to what about them is fact, and what is fable?"

"I hadn't thought about it."

"Like the Tree of Sorrows? That can't be real."

"The Tree of Sorrows?"

"Yeah, you had to have heard about that. You know, every three hundred nights, the Visitants- I mean, Klnovos- would choose a criminal, take them to the outermost region of their homeland, where the Tree of Sorrows grew."

"Why is that so hard to believe?" Orianne sighed, silently praying for another stretch of silence.

"They would tie the criminal to the trunk and dash them with rocks, and then forecast a meager or plentiful harvest based on how the blood flowed between the roots of the Tree- similar to how some Pathfinders and Wayfarers consult hen bones and palm fruit leaves before a voyage, or how the Searchers of the Vaincre would hang deserters and thieves from their trail markers. And if it were bountiful harvest, the tree would eat the criminal alive."

"I'm pretty certain that's not true."

"Oh, no, Kyrian and I used to make a game of it. On our journeys, when we'd pass a Vaincre trail marking, we'd try to guess what crimes the corpse had committed before being captured and hung."

"Not that." Orianne sighed again, "While the Klnovos may have executed criminals on the outer edges of their lands, I don't think they read the blood of the condemned. Also, the idea of a man-eating tree is beyond ludicrous."

"So is the thought of an Instructor walking alongside a shellskin, leading a bunch of Visitants—sorry, Klnovos-while farfadets fly overhead."

"Our situation is…unprecedented, yes." Orianne rolled her eyes, "But trees cannot eat men."

"Oui." Lanos chimed in, "It is a ridiculous rumor."

"Be that as it may, don't you think that it's based in some measure of truth?" Marie argued.

"The truth?" Lanos stopped and faced Marie, "The truth, small woman, is that instead of chasing knowledge, the majority of people choose instead to feed their ignorance. Most Javari don't even know the Klnovos' true name, how then could they have any knowledge of their cultural practices?"

"You have a point." Marie sheepishly replied.

"That is why my family left Courbonne. That is why I help the farfadets and shelter the Klnovos. That is why I am marching with you now, embarking on this dangerous excursion. Knowledge. To know why these terrible things have happened, so we can ensure they never happen again."

"I also use knowledge to ensure things don't happen again." Marie bragged, holding up a knife, "Knowledge of anatomy. Knowing just where to cut."

"Notice the path a few paces ahead." Orianne mercifully interrupted, "You can see the edge of the frost line, and there in the distance, the walls of the Outpost Cèdon."

Kiyolowe and her Sistren landed next to Orianne, Marie, and Lanos. The Klnovos gathered around and stared at the once busy road leading to the Outpost Cèdon. The pathway was a web of vines and roots. Fallen trees, covered in grey moss lined the edges of the path on either side.

At the edge of their sightline lay the spiked iron walls of Outpost Cèdon. The fort once rich with life, hopes, dreams and aspirations was now partially reclaimed by nature. Aside from the occasional bird call echoing off the cliff, the silence was sporadically broken by the soft murmurs of the coastal winds blowing through the abandoned structures.

Outpost Cèdon had hosted few esteemed or wealthy guests from Courbonne and had been kept afloat by Venturers and Pathfinders passing through on their journeys to chart the mysteries of Terre d'Os. As those excursions became increasingly infrequent, the residents of Outpost Cèdon sought out opportunities in Courbonne.

"There is no more tree cover." Orianne said to Kiyolowe, "Perhaps it'd be prudent for you and your Sistren to continue the journey on foot."

"Agreed." Kiyolowe confirmed.

Moving carefully around the dilapidated and cracked walls, climbing over dead trees and scattered vines, they made their way to the entrance. The Outpost was completely abandoned aside from the elements of nature that had confidently reclaimed the area. With its rusted rooftops, and spattering of crumbling, vine-covered walls defiantly refusing to succumb to their neglect, all signs of life had been lost to time. The spine-chilling atmosphere washed over Orianne and Marie.

"When you said there would be little resistance at the Outpost, I didn't think you meant it would be so desolate." Marie chuckled sarcastically.

"This isn't right." Orianne responded, "Outpost Cèdon is supposed to be manned by no less than twenty guardians at all times. We'll push on to Passerelle but mind your surroundings. Silence is not synonymous with safety."

"Did you feel that?" Kiyolowe asked. At first Orianne didn't know what she was talking about. But then she felt it, too. The breeze blew in from the coast, carrying the sweet damp smell as it brushed against her face, but there was a strong, yet subtle gust of air pushing against her sides.

There were loud quaking sounds and it seemed as though the earth was moving– like something was taking giant footsteps. Kiyolowe's six eyes widened. Muttering quickly in their strange, clicking tongue to her Sistren, the farfadets took flight, shooting up into the sky faster than an archer's arrow. The gusts of air felt stronger. Whatever it was, something was coming. Something large.

Orianne looked up at where Kiyolowe and her Sistren was circling. It seemed as though the leader of the farfadets was frantically pointing at something, just beyond the back wall. Orianne elbowed Marie and motioned in the direction that Kiyolowe had been pointing. They dashed towards the far wall, with the Klnovos following closely behind them.

They made it to the huge, heavy iron doors, the left of which hung at a twisted angle off the hinges. Stepping through, Orianne ignited her assegai, and Marie drew throwing knives in her good hand. Then they saw it.

The Klnovos who had been silent the entire journey, now spoke in fearful, indecipherable mutterings. Cedonia Barkridge, who seemed at the edge of death for most of the hike, now was electrified with the nervous apprehension. She hobbled to the front of the line, pushing her way between Orianne and Marie. Her elderly frame twittered with fear, and the horror loosened her bowels.

Cedonia's milky eyes grew faint as a shadow that was as wide as forty men standing horizontally with arms outstretched, rose, and blanketed the convoy. She raised her twitching arms reflexively, somehow hoping to block out the reality of what she was witnessing as the source of those strong, yet subtle gusts stood up fully into view. Her voice was hoarse, and barely audible, but Orianne, Marie, and all the Klnovos heard what she tearfully cried out.

"Breaker of boats! The Angel Queen!"

"What is she saying?" Marie whispered to Orianne, unable to take her eyes off the colossal creature just a few dozen paces in front of them.

"That creature should not be!" Orianne mumbled, "The last of them was killed by the Progenitors generations ago!"

"What is it?" Marie asked, gripping the Mournblade.

"Kongamato." Orianne managed a reply.

The Kongamato's long, thin head was buried beneath its outstretched left wing. The fist-sized eyes on either side were closed as the beast's muscular neck quivered methodically, preening the folds of tawny flesh between its shoulder joint and massive chest. Even with its head bent down, the kongamato was a shockingly impressive sight. Standing taller than two adult men, it flapped its gigantic wings as it groomed itself. Each swoop sending bulbous plumes of dust and dirt high into the air.

It hadn't yet seemed to notice the band of humans watching it clean itself, just a few dozen paces away. Blood drained for Orianne's face. The terrors of the mountainside massacre at the hands of the farfadets couldn't hold a candle to the atrocity before her. Horror churned in the pit of her stomach. Orianne diverted her gaze, careful to keep her focus instead on the gargantuan creature, lest she expel the contents and betray their tenuous position.

"There was no way to get around it without it noticing, and I don't think we are in a position to overtake it successfully through direct conflict." Kiyolowe whispered.

"Agreed." Marie nodded, whispering in reply, "Orianne, is there another way to Passerelle?"

"I don't believe so." Orianne responded fretfully.

"Can we double back through the Outpost?" Marie responded, "If we move quickly, we could avoid the beast, but I don't know if the elderly can manage the terrain."

"What if there are more kongamato lying in wait?" Kiyolowe sighed, "No, you must stay on the path forward."

"But how?" Marie whispered, "There's no way to pass."

"Then we will need to make a way." Kiyolowe replied, "I will take my Sistren and lead the Kongamato to the ranges of Ayrsulth. When it is safely lost among the peaks, we will rendezvous with you in Courbonne."

Kiyolowe spoke in a flurry clicking sounds to her Sistren, then the seven farfadets took to the skies. Flying high above the Outpost gate, they flew swiftly towards the kongamato with their heel spurs outstretched.

The kongamato raised its humongous head, quizzically watching the approaching farfadets with disinterest. The farfadets folded their wing and dove. They air whistled as they hurtled downward and slashed at the kongamato with their talons and heel spurs.

The wounds was superficial, but the intentions of the attack were successfully fulfilled. The kongamato was no longer disinterested. The kongamato unleashed a clamorous screech that reverberated off the crumbling walls of the outpost. With a single flap of its expansive wings, it took flight matching the altitude of the farfadets in a blink.

The farfadets headed for higher air. From the ground they resembled scattering mice, but there was a method to their chaotic exodus. They were leading the kongamato away from the Outpost back towards the hills of Ayrsulth.

"I hope they'll be okay." Orianne quipped, a concerned look draped over her tired face.

"What I don't understand," Marie began, "Is that you mentioned during your first encounter with farfadets, Kiyolowe transported you to their hive. Could she not have just teleported all of us past the fearsome creature, or perhaps teleported the kongamato, itself?"

"Maybe the kongamato is trop grand? Too big? Or perhaps there are too many of us?" Lanos shrugged, helping Cedonia to her feet.

"Whatever the reason, this plan seems to have worked." Orianne interjected, "But attacking Courbonne was going to be dangerous even with Kiyolowe and the Sistren. Now the first steps into the region will be ours alone."

"It went from a risky venture to a suicide mission." Marie quipped, "But if this is how I give my last breath, I vow to take the killer of Kyrian with me as well."

"I admire your dedication and determination, small woman." Lanos laughed, "I hope we can devise a strategy that we can all walk away from. But I do like the way you think, and I'm happy I have never been one of your tasks."

196

"Not yet at least." Marie teased, "You are from Courbonne after all, but I appreciate the compliment."

The convoy continued on, hiking for nearly a half day past the back wall of Outpost Cèdon, until finally, they came across the driftwood shanties and black mud shacks of the decrepit, yet beautiful enclave of Passerelle.

Built at the edge of the Sauvene Cliffs overlooking the inlet, Passerelle was the last refuge on the deserted plateau. The rustic charm of the dilapidated village lay in is unparalleled natural beauty. Coiling branches drooped from the sparse clusters of trees. Dazzling arrays of flowers added colorful, scented elements to the otherwise burnt amber hues of the rocky terrain.

A discord of wild noises seemed strangely synchronized with the repetitively rhythmic crashing of the waves and spattering of waterfalls pouring from the rockface below the edge of the cliffs. The foundations of the buildings were constructed right above the cascading spigots. The wind currents behaved oddly when the gales kissed the rushing torrents, enabling the ramshackle dwellings to withstand the otherwise cataclysmic storms.

"The kongamato must've come here before or after laying waste to the Outpost." Orianne remarked sadly, noting how just like the Outpost Cèdon, Passerelle had also been completely deserted.

"Must have." Marie agreed.

"Well, at least the buildings are still standing." Orianne said eyeing the accommodations, "Night fall is upon us. We should find shelter."

"See those two chimneys?" Marie pointed, "That building over there has enough room to hold us all, and it seems to be in decent shape. We can camp there, and then cross the inlet at first light."

The group headed in, stepping carefully over the cracked wooden slat of the central street. The puddles of murky water and thick mud reflected the same sense of desperation as the expressions on their weary faces.

"Pardon, Orianne." Lanos politely tapped Orianne's shoulder, "Before we make camp, perhaps you should familiarize yourself with this. Just in case we have any unexpected incidences during the night."

A heavy, scroll of well-worn parchment, bound by leather cord appeared in Orianne's hand. A dollop of white wax sealed the cord, and bore an inscription:

A Quarrel of Two Fought by Three

"What is this?" Orianne asked, "How did you…"

"For us to have any chance of survivor what we're planning to do, you must learn to wield Magyc." Lanos replied, "This scroll will instruct you on the First Five."

"Surely there is another." Orianne protested, "Cedonia, or one of the other Klnovos, perhaps?"

"They lack the strength to wield." Lanos shook his head, "But I see by your commendation markings, that many of your triumphs were academic accolades, oui? During Tutelage, I'm sure you read about the Magycs?"

"There wasn't much detail in what we were given to read." Orianne answered, "I am not from Courbonne."

"Your Stratum means nothing." Lanos cut her off, holding up his arm, "This arm was healed by Kiyolowe. But before, it was a twisted mess. I cannot wield the Magycs as I once had. We need someone stronger. Younger. Someone with honor. Someone that can be trusted. That someone is you. We need you to wield."

"I don't know." Orianne stared at the scroll, suddenly becoming very aware of the texture of the parchment against the palms of her hands.

"I'll do it." Marie stepped forward, "Teach me to the Magycs. I'll render the entire region of Courbonne to ash."

"With respect, small woman," Lanos smirked "From the little time we've spent together, I don't you need any Magycs to accomplish that."

"Truth." Marie smirked back, "I'm not much for reading anyway. I mean, I *can* read. But Orianne is much more inclined towards scholarly endeavors."

"But how do I…" Orianne ran her fingers along the cord binding the scroll.

"Ouvrez et lisez." Lanos calmed Orianne, "Open the scroll and read. The knowledge will come to you."

Orianne did as she was told. The words of the parchment were written in a language she didn't know, but somehow, she understood every sentence and phrase. It was strange and foreign, yet at the same time, comfortingly familiar. Viewing the text on the page felt like seeing portraits of ancestors. Her eyes were drawn to a phrase she instinctively understood to mean "maladie."

She folded the scroll and faced Marie.

"What's going on?" Marie asked taking a step back.

Orianne closed her eyes and concentrated. She threw her head back, and extended her left hand, with the palm towards the sky. She raised her right hand with her ring and small fingers curled beneath her thumb, her index and middle stretched out and one half clenched. She swung her right arm in a circle, drawing an invisible oval in the air.

Marie's gnarled stump throbbed as her shoulder began to quiver. Marie winced and dropped to one knee. The sensation of the beige-white humerus bone sprouting from the wound didn't hurt, but it wasn't pleasant. The humerus grew to the appropriate length, followed by the radius and ulna, and lastly the bones of her wrist, hands, and fingers.

The flesh of the stump quivered again. The muscles and arteries, veins and tendons spread over the bones, weaving through like grape vines on a garden trellis. A liquid coating of flesh drizzled down from Marie's shoulder, encasing the interior anatomy of the limb. Her arm was restored.

"Amazing!" Marie jumped to her feet and flexed her newly restore arm, "Lanos! Why didn't you do that?"

"Like I said, small woman," Lanos chuckled, "My abilities have been severely diminished. Tres bien! Very good, Orianne! Maladie is one of the most challenging wields of the Magycs!"

"How did I?" Orianne rubbed her head, "I need to—"

Marie caught Orianne as she lost her balance.

"Are you all right?" Marie asked, genuinely concerned.

"I'm fine." Orianne replied, "Just a little dizzy. But the scroll has given me another idea."

"Indeed. In due time." Lanos nodded to Marie, "Let's get her inside the building. She needs to rest. Wielding is not easy, but I've no doubt she'll learn how to cope."

-14-

Zamaya stood at the edge of her marquee tent and watched the sun rise, sipping rooibos tea from an ivory mug. She closed her eyes and took in pleasing tranquility of the dawn. She took another sip and glanced back over her shoulder, she laughed to herself softly as a worried smile spread across her lips.

The Bronze Chieftain's mutilated body lay on the plush rug next to her cot. The jagged edges of her cracked spinal column protruded through the wound. The corpse had stopped bleeding sometime in the night. The dwindling heat trapped in the flesh initially kept the scavenging vermin away, but now a multitude of insects and worms burrowed into the pulpy meat of the wound to feed on the soft tissue of her inner throat. Albert ran up the muddy path between the barrack tents and burst through the marquee tent door.

"Mother Zamaya. I have news to report!"

"Trouble with disposing of your courier scouts? I told you to move quickly. The chacal incantation does not leave a lot of time for hesitation once cast."

"No, Mother Zamaya. The courier scouts were bound securely before they began to transform, but I…is that the Bronze Chieftain's corpse?"

"Indeed, it is. The old sprite won't be a hindrance to our progression any longer. When we complete this expedition, we'll take the battalion to Courbonne and deal with the rest of the Chieftains and Elders. The people of Javari will finally be free." Zamaya smiled ominously

"Excellent, Mother." Albert bowed again.

"But that is not what you came to tell me."

"I saw farfadets and—"

"We are close to Ayrsulth. Seeing farfadets is not out of the ordinary for this region."

"They were being chased by your kongamato, so I--- "

"Excellent. It appears that after driving out the residents of the Outpost and village, the Miragem of the great monster still protects us. I'm surprised my wield has maintained so well. "

"Indeed." Albert bowed his head, "However during my descent, I noticed the light of a hearth coming from Passerelle. Finding it curious, I took a closer look."

"Survivors hiding from the kongamato?"

"That was my first assumption, but I crept to a window, and peered inside the silversmith's hut. I saw a dozen sleeping Visitants, surrounded by newly minted weaponry."

"Visitants?" Zamaya arched an eyebrow, "Are you absolutely certain it was Visitants?"

"Yes Mother." Albert nodded.

"An invasion?"

"Perhaps Mother, but most alarming was..."

"Yes?"

"I saw three from Javari.'"

"Prisoners of the Visitants?"

"I don't believe so. They were not bound or restrained."

"Could you identify them?"

"I did not recognize their faces, but it was a man of large stature, and two women, one of which- and this was most perplexing- bore the Mark of Three Moons."

"The Mark of Three Moons?" Zamaya kicked the Bronze Chieftain's corpse, " You clever old sprite. I underestimated you, Cossette."

"Mother?" Albert asked.

"Prepare my battalion for departure. Those in Passerelle cannot make any more progress. If word gets out that there are Visitants just across the inlet, there will be panic. They must be annihilated."

"As you have said it, so let it be so."

-TUTELAGE LESSON: THE MARK OF THREE MOONS-

The Mark of Three Moons is the oldest and most prestigious of commendation marks. Knowledge of the criteria by which one may earn The Mark of Three Moons is restricted to the highest echelons of authority and leadership: Skinners from the Vaincre Stratum, Venturers from the Explorateur Stratum, Dominies from the Enlightenment Stratum, and all of the Aristos of Unir Stratum -the Bronze Chieftain, the Iron and Gold Chieftains, the council of Elders, the Queenmothers and Chief Mentors.

Though the criteria is not widely known, eligibility and process for awarding the commendation are common knowledge. In terms of the former, any living person of Javari may receive The Mark of Three Moons. It is the only accolade that cannot be awarded posthumously. The process for receiving the commendation is as follows:

The highest-ranking member invites the recipient to join them for a private walk at first light. What they go and what is discussed are not public knowledge, but the "walk" last four days. When they return, the recipient now bears The Mark of Three Moons.

Perhaps the most notable bearer of The Mark of Three Moons is the Puissant Haute Champion of Javari, Zamaya Bellegarde, of the Vaincre Stratum. Prior to Zamaya Bellegarde, the previous twenty-one recipients of The Mark of Three Moons were Puissant Haute Champions: Julien Cochet, Flore Nicollier, Heath Bellsand, Reed Solidworth, Saffron Peacevale, Gervaise Didier, Maeve Passereau, Adriane Corriveau, Pleuris Wellthorn, Solenne Garret, Rebecca Crépin, Jeannine Chardin, Amandine Delisle, Elodea Nulifo, Antoinette Fuzile, Cousteau Zimiga, Alexandrine Kamisha, Regine Mdalla, Ashraf Benzema, Violette Grégoire Crépin, and Gabrielle Bennett.

Though there have been bearers from other Stratums, the number of Haute Champions has led many to believe the criteria for the honor is based in acts of valor in combat, or as a gift of thanks from the Chieftains, in response to a grand gesture or personal favor. This belief has not been definitively confirmed or denied by anyone, under charge of treason.

-15-

The unmistakable rhythmic swishing of leather and linen blended with the rustling clink of metal on suede as Erebus, Zamaya's elite warriors, marched through the abandoned streets of Passerelle. Having traversed the inlet before the moon fell, they arrived at the artisan village just as the final traces of the night sky had been ruptured by the broad fans of morning light spreading up and out over the horizon. The plumes of grey clouds shed the navy-blue cloak of evening to proudly display gleaming streaks of heavenly white.

The legendary battalion was divided into three divisions: The Stone, The Squall, and The Sacrée. The Stone took lead in all matters of violence, no matter how harrowing the assignment. Armed with swords, assegai, and bludgeons, it was said that if faced with a choice between facing a single member of The Stone or a float of hungry crocodiles, it would be wiser to face the latter.

The Stone were followed closely by The Squall. Dozens of specialists carrying slings, throwing clubs, and long spiked javelins. The Squall were as unwavering in their dedication to their craft, as they were to their leader.

Bringing up the rear were the cunning souls of The Sacrée. All were highly skilled in Magycs but limited the focus to specific wields. Half of The Sacrée are proficient in wielding Matryrr to conjure and cast devastating fires, while the remaining souls wielded Maladie, in order to mend injuries, no matter how severe. There would be no mercy. For Erebus, annihilation was the only acceptable outcome.

Erebus stopped at the silversmith's hut. The curved walls were built with burgundy bricks infused with ground sea glass, that sparkled in the midday sun. The iron shingles of the roof encircled a pair of towering chimneys.

The Stone drew their melee weapons and took up formation around the front and sides of the building. The Squall took up posts a few paces back, aiming their slings and spears at the windows. Behind them, The Sacrée ignited their fists in unison, casting the burning light of red and gold flames across the battleground.

The Stone dropped to their knees as The Sacrée cast a storm of enchanted fire, engulfing the silversmith's hut. The Squall squinted through the smoke, searching for any targets attempting to escape immolation.

The Sacrée let the fires burn for a moment longer, then cast the extinguishing wiled. The walls of the silversmith's hut were scorched but remained standing. The Sacrée pouted in disappointment. A soft chorus of mocking laughing bubbled amongst The Stone and Squall. As it was the hut of a smith, the walls had been insulated by layers of mineral wool as a safety measure, rendering their fiery opening assault useless.

The souls taking refuge inside the silversmith's hut, remained asleep, completely unaware that they were under siege by the finest killers in Javari. They didn't hear the hinges creak as the heavy mahogany door was slowly pulled open. They didn't hear the cautious steps and measured breaths of the melee warriors of The Stone as they entered the room, stepping over Cedonia as she lay curled against Lanos' muscular arms.

Skinner Kaleem Idrisi, the highest-ranking warrior of The Stone, and by extension, the leader of Erebus, surveyed his sleeping quarry and shook his head with a smirk. He leaned his assegai, Promise of Black across his shoulders. As the dense weight of the weapon pressed against the base of his neck, he relished the feeling of the spear's smooth iron shaft against his dry skin. The entire length of the staff was wrapped in Ndalawo pelts, allowing it to retain even the faintest traces of heat, which soothed his aching shoulders.

Kaleem looked over at Ninon, his second in command, and tapped his nose once, his forehead twice, then pointed back to the door. Ninon tapped her chin, nodded, and carefully made her way out of the building, to convey the message back to The Squall and Sacrée. There would be no need for a secondary wave of attack. The Stone would soon cleanse their weaponry with fresh blood.

Kaleem looked ventured further into the room, and spotted his target, a large man sleeping upright, with a small elderly woman nestled at his side, head tilted back against the stone pilasters of the central hearth.

Kaleem pulled Promise of Black off his shoulders and raised the serrated iron point to the supple flesh underneath the sleeping man's chin. Kaleem had made this kill innumerous times. The brief moment of resistance against the blade. The victim's shock of realization when the point effortlessly pierced their windpipe. The way the light faded from their pupils as the tip of the spear pushed through the throat, blocking the windpipe, severing the nerves, and slicing their neck bones as they drowned in their own blood. It was swift, silent, and effective.

Kaleem balanced the shaft of Promise of Black in the crook of his right elbow, and raised his left hand, with fingers outstretched. The other members of The Stone spread out across the room, readying their weapons.

Looking around the ensure that every slumbering body had a blade or club at its throat, Kaleem closed his left hand into a fist, and swiftly yanked down his arm.

With perfect, synchronized precision, the silver-grey blades were stained crimson. One hundred throats were punctured. One hundred arteries lacerated. The blood of the dead spurted and pooled, spreading the viscid fluid across the dusty tiles of the silversmith's floor.

Kaleem withdrew Promise of Black from the big man's throat. With a satisfied smile, he wiped the blade against his chest. The massacre was complete. Victory was absolute.

"Skinner Kaleem!" a harried whispered rang out.

Kaleem turned and frowned. Calipha held her weapon high, but the blade was still untouched by blood. Calipha was one of the more seasoned veterans of The Stone, but her age had not neutered her ferocity. Stepping over the leaking corpses, Kaleem made his way over to her.

"Why have you not completed your task?" the timbre of Kaleem's voice was tinged with annoyance. He had full confidence in Calipha's discretion, but there was nothing simpler than taking the breath from a sleeping target.

"With respect, Skinner, look at this girl." Calipha replied.

Kaleem inspected the still breathing woman at their feet. She wasn't very old but shouldn't matter. The Stone had massacred thousands of children without hesitation.

213

"Our orders were to take breath from those we find in Passerelle." Kaleem grumbled, his patience waning, "This girl is in Passerelle. Her breath must be taken."

"Indeed Skinner." Calipha explained, "But she bears The Mark of Three Moons. Is it not curious for a girl to be so highly decorated and lay here among Visitants?"

"Indeed, Calipha." Kaleem conceded, "This is most curious. Instead of taking her breath, render her unconscious then bind her limbs. We will present her to Mother Bellegarde"

-16-

Orianne tightened her cheek muscles against the irritating twinge filling her mouth and throat. She ran her tongue along a knot of rough, dry fibers and gagged.

"Orianne Duchamp." Zamaya pulled the knot of canvas out of Orianne's mouth. "I haven't placed eyes on you since The Ritual of Avenir. Look at how far you've come. I can hardly believe that you're not a Miragem."

"Zamaya Bellegarde." Orianne growled.

"This is Skinner Kaleem Idrisi, of Erebus." Zamaya tilted her head towards him, "Calipha, one of his champions. Calipha noticed your commendation markings and is the reason you still draw breath."

Orianne glared disdainfully at the very muscular, very dangerous man standing in the door. Zamaya waived her hand, silently instructing Kaleem to leave.

"You were traveling with Visitants." Zamaya's eyes darkened as she grabbed Orianne's chin, "Your intention was to invade Courbonne, and create chaos and carnage throughout the capitol, was it not?"

"My intention is to stop you." Orianne hissed.

The ropes binding her wrists burst into flames. Zamaya released Orianne's face and jumped back, startled by the sudden use of Magycs. The flames disintegrated the coils of twine and climbed up the center pole. Orianne ducked away reflexively, as the fire hungrily spread across and around the wooden pillar, singing the support lines.

"You wield Martyrr?" Zamaya exclaimed. Waving her hands, the flames vanished. "I didn't think the Bronze Chieftain would be so reckless."

"The Bronze Chieftain?" Orianne leapt to her feet and charged at Zamaya.

"Don't do that." Zamaya flicked her wrist, knocking Orianne backwards onto the floor of the tent, "Don't feign ignorance now. Who else did the Bronze Chieftain corrupt by bestowing powers upon those who do not understand?"

"I've never spoken with the Bronze Chieftain!" Orianne spat. Catching her breath, she pulled herself back to her feet defiantly, "Lanos Ndintu-Bel Acqwon gave me a scroll, and with it, the knowledge of Magycs."

"Ndintu-Bel Acqwon?" Zamaya's voice softened, "You claim to stand with an Ndintu-Bel Acqwon?"

"Not anymore" Orianne's voice remained fierce, "Erebus took his breath, just as they took the breath of a hundred Klnovos while they slept. You call them warriors. You call them champions? They are cowards!"

"Skinner Kaleem! Albert Eunice!" Zamaya bellowed. The timbre of her voice was an avalanche of otherworldly rage. Now it was Orianne's turn to be startled.

Kaleem and Albert rushed into the marquee tent. Both men dropped immediately onto the rugs covering the hard dirt floor and took a knee before Zamaya who eyed the two men with a pall unbridled infuriation cloaking her face.

"Skinner Kaleem?" Zamaya began.

"Yes, Mother."

"Was the breath of an Ndintu Bel-Acqwon taken?"

"I do not know, Mother." Kaleem responded, keeping his eyes toward the dirt, "Your word was to kill all we found in Passerelle. If an Ndintu Bel-Acqwon was in Passerelle, then they have given their last breath."

"Find Calipha." Zamaya placed her hand on Kaleem's head, "Inform her that she is to lead Erebus now. Her first act as Skinner is to retrieve the body of the Ndintu Bel-Acqwon, so they can be given a proper burial. That family has long fought for our cause and deserves our respect."

"As you have said it, so let it be so." Kaleem stood, nodded, and darted quickly out of the tent.

"Albert." Zamaya began.

"Yes, Mother."

"Why did you not tell me that it was an Ndintu Bel-Acqwon was sleeping among the Visitants?"

"I did not recognize that it was—"

"YOU DID NOT RECOGNIZE!!!!" Zamaya's voice exploded throughout the tent. Dozens of deadly puff adders materialized and swarmed over Albert. Orianne covered her ears and scooted back away from the swirling mass of vipers. "How is it that a man of Courbonne is a stranger to another from the same region! A stranger to one who works toward the same end!"

Albert's death wails filled the room. Dozens of fangs pierced every inch of his flesh. His veins filled with venom. Within seconds, the only thing left of Albert Eunice was the faintest echo of a scream wafting through the morning air. Zamaya waved her hands again. The snakes, along with the bloated corpse of Albert vanished.

"You kill so casually." Orianne muttered in disgust.

"I take no pleasure in it." Zamaya eyed Orianne curiously, "It's merely an unfortunate necessity. Taking breath is often the only way."

"The only way *you* know, perhaps."

"You have a bold tongue. Especially as you've just witnessed my comfort with taking breath."

"I will not hold my tongue for anyone. Not for Javari. Not for Klnovos. Not for you." Orianne proclaimed.

"So, you know the name Klnovos?" Zamaya smiled, genuinely impressed.

"I know many facts." Orianne scowled, "I know Klnovos have been forced from their homes. I know giant abominations roam the countryside. I know that monsters who were driven to extinction once again draw breath. I know the truth about the Progenitors. I know—"

"Truth? You claim to know truth?" Zamaya chuckled, "Tell me Orianne, did you know that the Progenitors and the Visitants are the same people, separated only by their method of transport, and time of arrival upon Javari shores? That the differences in physical appearances and societal practices are due entirely to environmental necessity, and a gulf spanning just a few hundred generations? You speak of all these souls as though they are disparate groups yet fail to see that Javari and Visitant are the same."

"They're called Klnovos."

"And we are called Javari. Our ancestors are called Progenitors. You are called Orianne. I am called Zamaya."

"Are you so corrupt that you hold no reverence for even the sanctity of names?" Orianne's jaw dropped.

"Are you so naïve as to believe names are deserving of sanctity?" Zamaya shot back, "It's a symbol, no different than The Mark of Three Moons we both wear on our faces. Removing the rings from our foreheads wouldn't diminish our skills. It wouldn't erase our history or accomplishments. You say Klnovos. I say Visitant. The value is not in the moniker, but rather what bears the moniker."

"But that…" Orianne searched desperately for a retort, but Zamaya's points were sound, "…makes a lot of sense."

"There are more worthwhile matters than names. Grave dangers that threaten all living souls. Not in the mountains of Terre d'Os, but right here in Terre de Sang. We quarrel amongst ourselves, giving credence to worthless divisions based on whim. Our leadership openly exploits these ludicrous fallacies, yet we refuse to accept that we have much in common with each other, and with the Klnovos, and with all the creatures of Terre d'Os. Much more than those sitting in the gilded halls of leadership. The Elders profit from all of our childish squabbling. The Chieftains laugh at our ignorance."

"Says the woman backed by the Bronze Chieftain!"

"The Bronze Chieftain is dead. I pulled out her throat, not two steps from where you now stand." Zamaya snapped, then quickly regained composure, "Orianne. I don't believe you are an agent of the Chieftains and Elders."

"I am a servant of Javari. I fulfill the promise of our ancestors, and the land of my birthright."

"Your birthright? Ten thousand generations ago our ancestors were banished to this land. It is not ours any more than the heat of the morning or dark of the night. They did not come by choice or destiny, but by way of horrors." Zamaya spat, "We cannot change what has already occurred, but we can *unbanish* our current state."

"That is also sound." Orianne frowned, surprised with how much she found herself agreeing with Zamaya.

"Indeed, it does." Zamaya smirked, "Do you know why I singled you out at The Ritual of Avenir?"

"You wanted me to pledge the Vaincre."

"The Chieftains wanted you to pledge the Vaincre." Zamaya pulled up a stool, and sat in front of Orianne, facing her eye to eye, "Based on reports of your progress, you were best among your peers—"

"And you wanted another killer for your cause."

"No. I've got plenty of killers. The Chieftains feared your intelligence. Had you been allowed to pledge the Enlightenment and stay in Navanca, their powers would've been threatened. A brilliant mind is more dangerous than a swinging blade. I was ordered to intervene to ensure that your gifts would be hindered by the arduous conditions of life traveling with the expeditions."

"You failed." Orianne snarled defiantly.

"Indeed, I did." Zamaya nodded and smiled, "Indeed I did. Just as I had hoped. Putting on that boisterous performance at the Ritual of Avenir would ensure that the mentors wouldn't questioned your Stratum assignment. Placing you with the most acclaimed and experienced Skinner, Hakim Jarrah, not only improved the odds of your survival, but it also made it politically untenable for the Chieftains to interfere. Just as our ancestors were banished, I banished you. And just as they turned atrocity into prosperity, you hold the potential to do the same. You wish to eradicate tyranny? You wish to liberate souls? You wish to bring about peace? Follow my plan, and you will."

"You speak of peace, yet you take breath from our people. You exploit our people. You manipulate our people. Your reasoning may be solid, but your methods undermine your intent." Orianne argued.

"Do not conflate pragmatism for malevolence. I was fighting in the Croyantes before you born. I've lived life as a scavenger, as a shellskin. I know what is truly necessary to survive, and what is merely desired. I know what is truly necessary to move the people, our people, all people, forward along the path of prosperity. I braided my own rope and climbed the mountain. And now that I'm here…" Zamaya trailed off, turning to stare out at the horizon.

"Now that you're here, you're pulling the rope, so that no other soul can ascend." Orianne's hands began to glow.

"No Orianne." Zamaya waved her hands dismissively, "I'm not pulling up the rope. There's no rope to pull. My plan is to level the mountain, so others won't have to ascend, but instead simply step forward."

Orianne leapt to her feet and braced herself for a quarrel. Zamaya remained seated on her stool, with her palms up, and a knowing expression draped across her exquisite face. Orianne dropped her fists and relaxed her shoulders. If Zamaya was telling the truth, she deserved Orianne's assistance and allegiance. If she was lying, she was far too skilled in wielding Magycs, for Orianne to do anything about it in the moment.

"Your plan to level the mountain, what does it entail?" Orianne inquired, sitting back down.

-17-

Skinner Kaleem Idrisi cursed as he traversed the inlet. Passerelle was not a lengthy journey, but repeating the same trip thrice in a day, like some common messenger, was beneath his station. How was he supposed to know that he was to spare the life of someone among a group of people he'd been ordered to kill?

He staked Promise of Black into the ground and took a knee to catch his breath. Just a few hundred nights ago, his body wouldn't have protested. The soreness in his joints were a painful reminder that he was no longer the spry combatant he once was. He brushed an errant dreadlock away from his face and caught his breath. Rubbing his bloodshot eyes, his mind overflowed with clever witticisms and brutal retorts to the relentless mockery that followed the announcement of his demotion.

He had been a fair leader. He had never been unnecessarily harsh with the warriors, but the culture of Erebus was built on hubris and posturing. Any perceived deviation from the rigorous tenets of virility were to be ridiculed without mercy- and they were. Kaleem stood and stared at his muddily obstructed reflection in the blood-stained blade of Promise of Black.

The red stripes under each eye marking his commanding station would soon be replaced by pairs of white lines denoting his relegation. When he was first honored with leading Erebus, he considered having the marks of command permanently etched into his cheeks. He sighed in relief that he hadn't. Calipha would've been bound by duty to have the tattooed flesh scraped off, so as not to diminish her authority. Instead, she merely had forced him to march fifty paces behind Erebus, so far back the rear line of The Sacrée wasn't even visible.

Deafening howls shook him out of his self-loathing. Squinting at the road ahead, Kaleem made out screeching shapes brandishing weapons advancing quickly. They ran without discipline, stumbling over the twisting vines and broken stones of the decrepit path. Jerking Promise of Black from the mud, Kaleem prepared for bloodshed. He laughed to himself at their chaotic buffoonery, wondering how this mob had slipped past Erebus.

They weren't soldiers. They were townsfolk. Kaleem had taken breath from angry mobs before. He had no qualms doing so again. Like so many who derived pleasure from cruelty, Kaleem's enjoyment of misfortune was purely vicarious. It was always better to deliver punishment rather than find yourself on the receiving end. He exhaled slowly, feeling his heartbeat accelerate with anticipation.

The wet thud of a disembodied hand landing in the mud at his feet increased the pounding of his blackened heart. More hands fell. Slowly at first. Then a dozen arms still gripping the hilts and handles of swords and clubs. The lower halves of twenty men. The shoulders and headless necks of thirty more. The sporadic trickle of airborne anatomy morphed into a downpour of butchery.

Kaleem squatted into a ball, dropping his head between his knees for protection. Gradually, the limbs and organs stopped raining. Kaleem raised his eyes to watch the severed head of Calipha roll to a stop an arm's length away. Kiyolowe and her Sistren touched down in front of him, turning his anxious disquietude.

"The Doyenne!" Kaleem stuttered.

"Kaleem Idrisi," Kiyolowe's voice rang through the chambers of his mind, "You are a vile and remorseless brute. Your death will be of no great loss."

"My orders were to take breath, and taking breath is what I shall do!" Kaleem gulped, scrounging the pit of his gut for the last remnants of courage, he lunged the great spear forward.

Kiyolowe grabbed the spearhead and yanked it free from Kaleem's grasp. She tossed the weapon to her Sistren, who took Promise of Black to the skies.

"I think not." Kiyolowe responded, slashing open both of his forearms with a single swipe of her talons.

Kaleem dropped to his knees as the Klnovos arrived at the banks of the inlet and encircled him. Lanos pushed his way to the front and leaned over Kaleem.

"Allo, man of Erebus." Lanos' voice was ominous, "Tu es en dernier. You must be the last. We already had the pleasure of meeting your brothers in Erebus."

"No!" Kaleem grunted maniacally, "I plunged Promise of Black into your neck and ripped out your throat myself!"

"Ah." Lanos chuckled again, "I'm afraid that was the Miragem. Many of us, myself included, believed that wielding Miragem to mask our slumber was overly cautious. But when we saw Erebus stabbing away at our false manifestations? Well, wow. I am very embarrassed to have doubted her. In retribution for your attempted massacre, Klnovos took breath from Erebus."

"Very clever." Kaleem conceded, "But not too cunning. Why wield Miragem for everyone but the woman with the mark?"

"She's a novice. She had to be close to make the wield sufficiently convincing." Lanos shrugged with a wry smile.

"Understood." Kaleem raised his chin, "I am Skinner Kaleem Idrisi, commander of Erebus, and faithful servant of Zamaya Bellegarde. I give my last breath to you."

"Keep your breath. I am an Ndintu Bel-Acqwon. I am a protector. I am a provider. Besides, you are severely wounded and greatly outnumbered. I defend Klnovos, but I am not a merciless killer."

"I am." Marie called out, as the Mournblade whizzed past Lanos' shoulder.

The massive knife split Kaleem's head in two. Kaleem fell facedown forward into the mud. The Klnovos averted their eyes, but there was no escape from the nauseating squelch of the Mournblade being wrenched from Kaleem's corpse that filled their ears.

"You didn't have to do that." Lanos chastised Marie.

"No, you're right." Marie shrugged wiping chunks of brain from swedge- the beveled area along the spine of the Mournblade, "I didn't have to do that. But I wanted to. And there will be a lot more blood to shed when we reach Courbonne. Now let's go retrieve Orianne."

-18-

"There will be no Stratums. No Javari or Visitants. No Terre de Sang or Terre d'Os. There will be only the living and the dead. True equity to bring about true prosperity. My position not only allows me access to power of our rulers, but to siphon that power, and use it against them." Zamaya explained, barely hiding her pain and passion.

"How so?" Orianne scrutinized Zamaya's every syllable.

"The Chieftains and Elders had been corrupting the Magycs. They know as well as I do- and as you are becoming aware- that the divisions of the people are asinine. They also know that if enough of the Javari, Visitants, and creatures of Terre d'Os realize this, the era of subjugation will come crashing to an end. The lone ant can be trampled. A but a colony of ants can take down a lion."

"Do you have proof of their corruptions?"

"People want passion, not proof."

"People need proof."

"I envy your idealism." Zamaya chuckled, "Just four or five-thousand nights ago, the Elders hired a special latrine-master, tasked with placing barley seeds in the toilets of Courbonne families. He would check the seeds during his rounds, and if they sprouted, he would report back to the Elders, who would then use Magycs to snatch life from wombs, before the mothers even knew they were with child. They took these unborn, invisible specks of life, turned them into chacals. Do you know what happened when the people discovered this?"

"What?"

"Nothing. Without even holding a trial, the tribunal magistrates ruled the matter slander without merit, and the Chieftains outlawed further discussion. That latrine-master? He still in his position now."

"Oh no!" Orianne was shocked by the story, but even more shocked that she trusted Zamaya so readily.

"A generation purloined wanders the wastelands of Terre d'Os, offsetting the natural balance thanks to the nefarious malevolence of the Chieftains and Elders. Not that they held any reference for the natural. They conjured an enormous carcolh to roam the forests. I believe you encountered the beast of which I speak?"

"Yes." Orianne hung her head.

"I'd nearly forgotten that your aversion to violence extends to animals. A carcolh that size doesn't relegate itself to the forest. It doesn't relegate itself to anything. I had to conjure the something to keep the carcolh away from crossing into Terre de Sang."

"The kongamato!" Orianne's eyes widened as she began to put the pieces together, "Why didn't you call them out when you discovered their crimes? Chieftains and Elders are not above the reach of the tribunals."

"For the same reason you do challenge me now." Zamaya smiled knowingly, "My opponent is nigh indomitable. Victory will not come challenges in the courts any more than it would come quarreling in the streets."

"Then what?"

"Settle not for victory when triumphant is at hand."

"I don't know what that means…" a sharp pain burst across Orianne's chest, pulsing outward from the old wound she'd acquired during Tutelage. Orianne grimaced through the searing agony.

"Why are you holding your chest in that way?" Zamaya asked genuinely concerned. She reached out, her eyes were almost maternal, "Here. I'll wield Maladie and alleviate your pains. Take it as a token of trust."

"Orianne Duchamp!" Kiyolowe's voice whispered through Orianne's mind, "Take cover!"

"No! Wait!" Orianne covered her head and ducked as the support lines and roof beams at the top of the marquee tent splintered and snapped beneath the weight and talons of Kiyolowe and her Sistren.

Crashing down through the ceiling, the Sistren landed in front of Orianne. Gathering in a protective circle, they extended their leathery wings around her.

Kiyolowe slammed down on top of Zamaya. Her venomous heel spurs slashed the Puissant Haute Champion's tendons, shredding her shoulders. The leader of the farfadets thrashed her heavy tail, lacerating Zamaya's thighs. The ruptured arteries coated the walls of the marquee tent with warm crimson and mortal fear.

Orianne peaked between the folds of the Sistren's wings. Kiyolowe stood over a broken and bloodied Zamaya. Kiyolowe reared back to deliver the killing blow.

"Kiyolowe! Read her thoughts!" Orianne screamed.

Zamaya parted her lips. Between bloody coughs and gurgling attempts to draw breath, she managed a barely audible series of staccato clicks. Kiyolowe folded her wings and lowered her talons. Zamaya made clicking sounds again. Kiyolowe motioned to the Sistren. They withdrew their wings and made space for Orianne to step forward.

"She speaks in your tongue?" Orianne gasped, "What does she say?"

"Truth." Kiyolowe addressed Orianne, but kept her eyes locked on Zamaya, "She says she wants you to find the truth. She claims to be wearing the Veil of Bone, and wants you to take it, and use it to reveal the truth to all the living souls of Javari. What is this Veil of Bone?"

Kiyolowe's sentence hung in the air as the light faded from Zamaya's eyes as she quietly gave her last breath. a blinding light filled the marquee tent. Zamaya's remains- her skin, her hair, her jewelry, and clothing- crumbled into a fine red powder, leaving behind the most exquisite garment Orianne had ever seen.

The threads of the textile were so impossibly delicate, she could see through it to the multi-colored pattern of the rugs below. Orianne forced herself to maintain her stare. Mesmerized both by the beauty of the Veil, and the impossibility of its existence.

Orianne picked up the Veil. Grunting at the paradoxical weight, she slipped it over her shoulders. The enchanted fabric felt as though she were wearing a cloud of fog. The fibers passed through her clothing, into her pores.

The halls of Orianne's mind were flooded with images and sounds, a torrent of knowledge overwhelmed her senses. The entire experience lasted slightly longer than the blink of an eye, but to Orianne, she had bore witness to the origination and cessation of existence.

"Is everything all right?" Kiyolowe asked apprehensively approaching Orianne.

"No Kiyolowe, everything is not all right. The marked child, Zamaya Bellegarde is dead." Orianne replied, "The creatures of Terre d'Os face extinction. The Elders and Chieftains in Courbonne still hold dominion over Javari and Klnovos alike through fear and subjugation, and they have ten million warriors at their disposal."

"Ten million warriors?" Kiyolowe scoffed, "How are we going to stop ten million warriors?"

A long black tail curled out from underneath Orianne's tunic brandishing a flaming assegai. Her eyes flashed red and gold. A geyser of red and gold flames erupted from her hands. Kiyolowe shielded her six eyes as the coiling tongues of blue-black smoke encircled her, Orianne, and the Sistren.

The enchanted blaze burst from the center of Orianne's chest wound, instantly rendering the canvas walls and wooden pillars to ash. The spherical wall of flames swelled and crested above the treetops, washing throughout the valley and across the inlet. The fiery waves flooded the regions. The cities and estates of Courbonne, the villages and towns of Navanca and Tolerbella, the hamlets and parishes of Ardwood, every soul drawing breath was bathed in the red and gold inferno that outpaced the wind, consuming everything in its mystical wake.

The ocean of fire dissipated. Kiyolowe opened her eyes, blinking in the unfiltered morning light glistened off of her skin, as a chill of anxious anticipation trickled down her spine. Orianne smiled serenely.

Kiyolowe entered Orianne's mind. Javari and Klnovos alike gathered in their respective streets. In every settlement, every living soul stood united in purpose, their minds filled with the knowledge of truth carried on that wave of Magyc fire. Some marched towards the Elders and Chieftains of their towns, eager to punish them for their crimes. Some took out the weapons holds and symposiums, while others descended upon the banks. The jacquerie covered the entire continent without exception.

For every ten hands wielding a blade of revenge, there were a hundred hands wielding tools to rebuild. For every hundred instances of rebellious bloodshed, there were a thousand instances of righteous demonstration. From the hills of Ayrsulth and wilds of Umadyn, Magyc creatures, predator and prey, sentient and feral, embarked upon a mass exodus, crossing the border between Terre d'Os and Terre de Sang for the first time in over a thousand generations.

"Knowledge, Kiyolowe." Orianne smiled, "We will still face obstacles. We will still suffer tribulations. But through knowledge, we will be both victorious and triumphant."

"As you have said it, so let it be so…"

ABOUT THE AUTHOR

T. Aaron Cisco is a Minneapolitan by way of Chicago. His favorite game is chess, his favorite color is grey, and his favorite movie snack is dark chocolate Raisinets…

Made in the USA
Middletown, DE
18 July 2023